Katharine Leslie

Sentenced to fourteen years' imprisonment for a theft of which she is innocent, sixteen-year-old Katharine Leslie finds herself in Newgate, friendless except for Michael Edes, a young doctor. Through his help and her own daring she escapes to America, determined to find the security she longs for in the household of Edmund Winter, a wealthy Tory merchant.

But time and events move too swiftly for her. Caught up in the bitter strife between Tory and rebel, she struggles to find her place in a world of turbulent ideas and actions where the familiar patterns are broken and her own values must change. Based on actual incidents in Revolutionary history in Falmouth, Maine, KATHARINE LESLIE is a gripping and romantic tale, high lighted by sensitive black-and-white illustrations by Polly Bolian.

Katharine Leslie

by Audrey White Beyer

illustrated by Polly Bolian

ALFRED A. KNOPF / NEW YORK

L. C. catalog card number: 63-9110

THIS IS A BORZOI BOOK,
PUBLISHED BY ALFRED A. KNOPF, INC.

Copyright © 1963 by Audrey White Beyer

First Edition

In love and gratitude to
my father, William Joseph White,
and my mother, Hermon Brand White,
who came to Falmouth and made it their home

Author's Note

The story of Katharine Leslie is entirely fictitious. But the picture of the world she lived in is not exaggerated. *The State of Prisons in England and Wales* (1777) by John Howard bears witness to the wretched conditions in Newgate and other prisons of eighteenth-century England. So do the studies of more recent authors.

The burning of Falmouth (now Portland, Maine) occurred on October 18, 1775. The journals of the Reverend Thomas Smith and the Reverend Samuel Deane describe this event, as do the histories of Portland written by Nathan and William Goold, and William Willis.

General Jedidiah Preble, Captain Henry Mowat, Captain Samuel Coulson, Sheriff William Tyng, the Reverend John Wiswall, and Colonel Thompson of Brunswick were men of flesh and blood, who, in accordance with their beliefs and convictions, contributed to the history of their time.

1 {

Even now, thrust hard against the narrow seat of the coach that slewed over the muddy road toward London, Katharine Leslie found it hard to believe the nightmare real. Surely if she opened her eyes— But her eyes were open. She stared down at her gray gown, the modest, unobtrusive uniform of the governess—seeing its folds dirtied at the hem, its overskirt streaked with grime. When she lifted her eyes to the English countryside, stretching bleak and damp beneath a dripping sky this February day of 1774, every tree and hedge and frozen field stood out in cold reality. Putting her face up to the coach window, she could feel the wind probe beneath the casing, as it drove the rain in icy splinters against the glass. She could feel, too, with each lurch of the coach, the iron fetters that bound her ankles. This agony was real enough.

No, this was no dream. This was nightmare—threatening, tumbling fantasies, alive and genuine. The guard, tipsy, blasphemous, swaying on the outside seat and regaling the driver with ribald stories, might have been Charon guiding her to Hades, the coach his boat to the lower world. And only the deep recesses of the earth could harbor such cold as this, she reflected with a shiver. Even the chill of the county jail—her shelter for the past three weeks—had yielded a little warmth from a fire of green twigs. But the coach offered no such fitful comfort. And Newgate? Her breath came sharp in her throat at the thought of her destination. There was no reason to suppose she would find the London prison more bearable.

As they rolled on toward the city, the rain gradually let up, and in the distance now she could see the smoke of many chimneys. Black and spiraling, it seemed to draw down the clouds in darker masses. But here and there a church spire pricked the murky sky, and the dome of St. Paul's stood out sturdy and bold. As she shifted her gaze back to the muddy road, the coach ground to a stop, and in a moment the guard appeared at the door.

"Ye can git down." He balanced precariously, gazing at her out of rheumy eyes. "We're stoppin' here a while." Clumsily he let down the step, and she saw that they had drawn up in an innyard.

"Please—" She heard the note of pleading in her voice and was ashamed of her weakness. In stronger tones she began again. "Is—is there no way you can remove my—my shackles?"

"No." His eyes slid away from her and riveted upon a wheel. "No, there ain't."

The coach step was high, and she managed to reach it. But the leap to the ground was so steep, and the arm offered her so unsteady, that her hobbled feet brought her crashing to her knees. As she fell, the irons bit viciously into her flesh, and faint with pain, she knelt a moment until her breath returned. Time was, she thought bitterly, when, bruised ever so slightly, she would have been swiftly comforted in the strong arms of the young master of Blaize House. Jay would have raised her up and offered tender words. Now the knight at hand swayed away toward the horses, leaving her to gain a footing in the dirty innyard as best she could.

"Wretch!" she muttered angrily, outraged at his indifference. Too proud to beg assistance, Katharine struggled to her feet, adjusted her bonnet with trembling fingers, and rearranged her shawl. Then she shuffled to the door of the inn, hearing the telltale chain clang on the brick floor as she moved over the threshold, feeling the warm air gush round her in welcome waves as she came into the long, dim room.

A large woman in a white mobcap and apron turned

from serving a guest and came toward her. Her sharp glance took in Katharine's plight immediately.

"Ye'll find all ye'll need for comfort in that room yonder. Water and soap's tuppence."

"*Hot* water?" The girl's blue eyes widened, her black lashes sweeping upward in astonishment.

"If ye want, but it'll cost extra."

Katharine thrust out her hands, black with the mud of the yard. "For hot water and soap, I would give you my last penny," she said grimly. Gingerly she drew a small purse from the pocket of her gown and dropped several coins into the landlady's palm. "Bring me as much as you can spare, if you please."

"Ye'll want something to eat," the woman suggested shrewdly. "Food's not free."

"No." Stifling the pangs of hunger, tenacious now under the redolent odors of the inn, the girl shook her head. "No, thank you. I cannot afford both. The water will have to suffice."

"As ye will." The woman left her, and Katharine opened the door into a small room fitted up for the comfort of travelers.

Removing her bonnet, she shook out her dark hair, and then, lifting her skirts, examined her bruised ankles. Where the bands had dug into her flesh, ugly brown stains showed on her tattered stockings. These new marks almost perfectly matched the stylish clocks she had embroidered up the sides of her white hose a few weeks back. What an irony that the stockings so carefully embellished to catch the admiring glance of the young Lord Blaize should now bear the bloody marks of leg irons!

With a warning word the landlady entered, carrying a large tin of hot water. Carefully she set it down and then turned to face Katharine.

"The gentleman dining says he would count it a privilege if ye would be his guest at dinner," she said shortly.

The girl started. She had been only dimly aware of a guest in the dining room. Now her eyes darkened as they met those of the older woman in puzzled inquiry.

"Surely he cannot realize I am"—she paused, then emphasized the ugly words deliberately—"a convicted thief?"

"What's the difference? The dinner's good—chicken and dumplings that I cooked myself." As if Katharine's hesitation were a personal affront, her voice sharpened. "There'll be nothin' like it in prison, believe me!"

"I do believe you," Katharine answered in sober tones. "And I *am* hungry." From a complete stranger this gesture of friendliness seemed unbelievably kind, and suddenly it was more than she could bear. Her voice broke, close to tears. "My—my thanks to the gentleman, if you please. Say that I will join him when —when I have completed my toilette."

She scrubbed her face and neck and hands, and then with reckless abandon poured fresh water into the basin and thrust in her hands again, reveling in the hot, soapy suds and the delicious warmth that crept up her arms. Water—*hot* water! And food! The combination was intoxicating. To be sure, there had been bread and a cup of tepid tea before she started on her journey. But now—the promise of a feast! Too late she realized that she had not bargained for a towel. But she dared not spend another penny. With the edge of her shawl she dried herself, then combed her dark locks, catching them up from the nape of her neck with a bit of ribbon. In the looking glass above the commode her face was pale and clean, she saw with satisfaction, a pleasing contrast to her torn and rumpled gown. Was the stranger young or old? she wondered suddenly. Not that it mattered. He had offered her food. Draping the shawl over one arm and catching up her bonnet, she moved into the dining room, the chain rasping incongruously along the brick floor. Hearing it, Katharine stiffened and raised her head higher. Though she was branded a thief, she would not cower like one.

The gentleman had risen as she approached, and now in the light of a blazing fire, she saw him plainly. A tall, well-built young man, he was dressed in riding clothes, booted and spurred. The coat was rather shabby, she noticed, but he wore it with an easy grace. His black hair was clubbed back in a queue—he wore no wig— and his face, sharp-boned, tanned, could almost be called handsome, with its firm chin and generous mouth. Was he twenty—twenty-five? Somewhere between, perhaps.

"Michael Edes, your servant, ma'am." Taking her hand, he bowed, and Katharine contrived a slight curtsy. "I am greatly in your debt," he added with a smile. "You save me from the misery of dining alone."

Although his tone was light and his gestures easy, she saw the compassion in his dark eyes as he helped her to a seat opposite him near the fire. Acutely aware of her disordered apparel, she was grateful for the graceful manners that could ignore her fetters and accept her as an equal.

Striving to keep the light note, she met his eyes with a smile. "Indeed, it is I who am indebted to you, sir. You rescue me from the pangs of overwhelming hunger!"

He laughed, and at once served her with generous portions before refilling his own plate. Immediately Katharine's interest flew to the food as she savored the tender breast of chicken and the hearty dumplings smothered in gravy. How good it was! Not since Blaize House had she tasted such fare, and there, for the governess at least, such an abundance as this was rare indeed.

"Inn food is always a gamble," her host said as he cut and buttered a slice of the fresh bread and offered it to her. "But here the landlady boasts justly of her fare, I think."

"To me this seems like food for the gods," she answered earnestly, biting into the delicious bread crust.

"And like the gods I am using it as a bribe," he answered with a slight smile.

Startled, she looked up to meet his gaze, cool and level with her own. "You are bribing *me?*" she exclaimed in bewilderment.

"I am trying to, at least. Oh, do not be alarmed, I beg you!" He was swiftly reassuring. "I want only a seat in your coach—a ride back to town. My horse went lame about a half mile from here. I had been called into the country to visit a patient. I am a physician, you see, and I must be in London tonight."

Katharine put down her fork, and with nervous fingers crumbled a bit of bread on her plate. "The—the coach belongs to His Majesty's Government." Not trying to soften the harsh facts, she plunged on. "It is used for the transportation of criminals from one place to— to another." She felt her face flame, but she looked up resolutely as she finished. "Unfortunately I have no authority over who shall ride in it."

"But you do not object to a companion?"

"No." For a long moment she studied him, seeing the clean shirt and freshly laundered neckcloth so in contrast with her own soiled garments. The irony of his request forced her to a wry smile. "If you do not object to me as a companion"—she gave a deprecatory glance at her own wretched attire—"how could I possibly object to you?"

"Then if you will pardon me a moment, I'll make

arrangements with the driver." He rose and disappeared toward the kitchen.

Katharine returned to her food, hurrying a little now. With a bit of bread she mopped up the gravy, then quickly downed another helping of chicken. Her glance swept the room, making sure it was empty, before she slipped the rest of the bread deep in her pocket. How sly she had become these last weeks—and how greedy! A ride in the coach was little enough to ask in payment for a meal as delicious as this, she thought, and a companion to talk to would be pleasant. He seemed a gentleman. Yet what he was—doctor, footpad, highwayman—did not really matter. Fetters changed one's views as well as one's company, she reflected. And beggars could not be choosers.

He was back. "We leave in about five minutes," he said easily. "Just time enough, I think, for you to finish that apple tart."

While she hastily devoured the tart, her companion pulled on a riding cloak and picked up a small bag from the floor. Then, seeing that she was finished, he pulled out her chair, offering her his arm. With a hand on his sleeve, she moved across the room, feeling the drag of the chain, and more sharply, the painful chafing of the irons.

Clean straw made a path to the coach. The driver was at the horses' heads, and standing stiffly by the step, obviously sobered by food and rest, was the guard.

Michael Edes ignored him with a scarcely concealed

scorn that convinced Katharine he had witnessed her humiliating arrival.

"Keep your feet together and your head down, if you please," he ordered, and in one deft motion he lifted her onto the coach seat. Across the floor boards, too, the straw was fresh and clean, she saw now, and she turned to him quickly as he entered.

"You have wrought miracles indeed!" She tried to laugh, but though his swift help had diminished the pain of the shackles, the agony they caused with every step had not been entirely alleviated, and she sank back against the seat with a grateful sigh. "Surely my ascent was more graceful than my descent from this hateful vehicle," she murmured, looking up at him with a twisted smile.

"I should hope so. Clumsy, blundering oaf that he is!" His glance swept outward to the seat where the guard now sat with the driver. Then, as the coach lurched to a start, he turned to her with a shrug and a half-smile. "Well, we are in their hands. May heaven protect us!"

Warmed by the inn fire, Katharine felt the wind more sharply now as it probed beneath her shawl, and she shivered.

"Have you no cloak?" he demanded, his glance sweeping her. "Nor gloves nor pattens?"

"They disappeared in jail," Katharine confessed.

"Merciless thieves." Drawing off his gloves, he dropped them in her lap. Then he pulled off his cloak.

"Here, take this. And pull the capes well up around your shoulders," he ordered brusquely, helping her into it.

"But you," she exclaimed. "I cannot——"

"I shall be perfectly comfortable without it. Do as I say, if you please."

With no further protest she settled the heavy folds of the riding cape around her, then thrust her hands gratefully into the warm gloves.

"How do your ankles feel?"

She recognized the physician speaking and answered without embarrassment. "They are swollen and chafed, of course."

"I saw that as I lifted you in. When you come to Newgate, have the turnkey strike off the shackles at once. Pay him any price he demands, but get rid of them. If you can bathe the sores they have caused, do so." From his bag he brought out a small jar. "And use this ointment. It may help."

"You are very kind," she murmured, slipping the jar into one of her pockets.

"How much money have you?"

"Enough," she replied hastily.

"How much?"

Removing a glove, she drew out her purse and emptied its contents into her other hand.

"As I thought. That amount will scarcely see you through the gates. Dear God!" he exclaimed harshly.

"If children must be sent to prison, cannot someone at least provide for them?"

"I am sixteen," she replied with dignity. "Hardly a child!"

"Sixteen!" Falling back against the seat, he said no more, but sat staring out of the coach window, his face moody and implacable.

They rode on in unhappy silence. Katharine could feel his outrage, yet she was aware, too, that it was roused by the circumstances rather than by herself. A warm gratitude welled within her. To have someone—anyone—righteously wrathful on her account was a new and poignant experience. Striving to break the constraint between them, she ventured on a new topic of conversation.

"Are you a Londoner by birth, sir?" she inquired courteously.

"So we are to observe the amenities in polite conversation." He turned toward her, a flicker of laughter in his eyes. "I see that you have indeed been well brought up. No, ma'am, I am not a Londoner. I was born in England, to be sure, but my parents died when I was very young. I grew up the ward of an uncle in America." The anger was gone, and the lines of his face had softened under the caress of memory. "My home is in the Province of Maine, a part of the Colony of Massachusetts. I grew up there in a small town called Falmouth, over a hundred miles northeast of Boston. You won't have heard of it."

"I've heard of Boston certainly," she retorted quickly. "It's the place where the rebels threw the King's tea into the water."

"Yes, bless their hearts! Giving the King back his own with interest!" His laugh was one of pure delight, and she turned amazed eyes on him. He met her glance. "Ah, but I shock you," he said, gently mocking, "loyal subject that you are—though in chains."

Desiring any conversational topic but herself, Katharine pressed on. "But how come you to be in London, sir?" she asked.

"After completing my studies at Harvard College, I came to London to study medicine at the Royal College of Physicians. Now I am an associate—no, let us be honest—really a lackey for the famous Doctor Ashby. I call on his out-of-town patients, ladies with the vapors, gentlemen with gout. I charge exorbitant fees—most of which go to the good Doctor Ashby. And I return from the country to London, as I am doing now, to start the whole round all over again."

In his eyes and in his voice the self-mockery was evident. Seeing it, Katharine spoke more carefully. "You do not enjoy your work then?"

"Do not misunderstand me. I love my work," he said firmly. "Sometimes I am of real help, especially in the prisons and with the poor. But the system I am involved in now—I cannot regard it as strictly honest. And London society is dissolute. While the politics—" He shrugged. "The politics, except for Burke and Chatham, are discouraging indeed. These last six months I've watched the King's friends go further and further toward stifling every breath of life out of the American colonists."

"But the Americans! The colonists!" she exclaimed, astounded at his point of view. "Surely they must be punished?"

"Why?" he demanded. "Because they dare to stand up for what they believe is right?" His glance went to her shackles. "Tell me, ma'am, just what will your punishment prove? That Lady Blaize was justified in calling you guilty?"

Katharine flinched. The quick thrust had taken her unawares. For a few moments she had almost managed to forget her destination—Newgate, prison of felons and debtors. Now this stranger flung her abruptly back to the present. She looked at him in bewilderment. "How—how do you know so much of me?" she stammered.

"You forget that there are journals and papers—and people talk. No one proved that you stole that emerald brooch, only that it was found in your room. Oh, I don't count the testimony of that terrified little chambermaid," he added scornfully, "even if his Lordship, the judge, did." He looked at her more closely. "You, I understand, refused from the very first to call yourself a thief."

She nodded.

"Yet it's said that her ladyship offered you immunity and a promise not to bring charges—provided you confess and leave her household?"

"Yes," she whispered.

"Little fool." Harsh though the words were, the tone was surprisingly gentle. "Why didn't you accept her terms?"

"I have my good name!" Her anger blazed up. "It's *all* that I have! And I am not a thief. Why should I say I am?"

"To save yourself. There is no better reason."

She was silent. He had touched on the decision she had come to debate in every waking hour. There had been no question in her mind at first. She was innocent. And because she was innocent, she had dared to be resolute, to put her faith in the justice of the courts. She had reckoned, too, that Jay would hasten to her defense, declare his love for her in public as he had in private. Here, she knew to her sorrow, she had been more than innocent—she had been a fool. For the young master of Blaize House had said nothing. This denial, more than anything else, had strengthened her determination to save her good name. Injured pride had bolstered her courage. She had refused to confess to a crime she had not committed. She had refused to give Lady Blaize the satisfaction of holding her up to her son as a thief. But on the accusation of a powerful woman, and the damning testimony of an ignorant maid, the judge had condemned her. Now she was on her way to prison. Had she confessed, she might be free.

She turned to Michael Edes, a new thought bursting in her brain. Could the verdict have been modified? Was the young doctor bearing some sort of pardon? Katharine's heart leaped, and her voice trembled as she spoke.

"Have you been sent to—to———"

"No." The word was quick and brutal. "I am no servant to the courts and no friend to Lady Blaize, though I attended her once some time back. I saw you that autumn day in the garden with young Blaize. Oh, do not look so hopeful!" he cried in a harsher tone. "I bear no last-minute reprieve. Would to God I did!"

Katharine sank back, hope trickling away. Yes, she thought numbly, there had been tender scenes in the garden. Had Michael Edes witnessed one of these? Had Lady Blaize? And in the garden, withered and browned by the breath of December, had come the final repudiation that she recalled now in all its ugliness.

"If I do not confess to the theft of the brooch, your mother threatens to bring charges against me!" she had cried out in terror, clinging to Jay that winter morning.

"Then confess, in God's name!" In angry impatience he had flung away from her. "What difference does it make?"

Staggered by this callousness, she stared up at him in bewilderment. His stocky figure in its handsome cloak blurred before her eyes, and her voice, when she found it, came no more than a whisper.

"Jay! You—you said——"

"I know very well what I said," he exclaimed petulantly. "A few foolish words no kitchenmaid would take seriously!"

Slowly her breath came under control, her vision cleared, and she saw him as he was.

" 'I love you,' is not 'a few, foolish words,' " she answered quietly. "And if you feel they are, I now release you from your promises." Then outrage, hot and searing, flamed within her. "But I shall not confess to being a thief!" she cried passionately. "Never! Why, one of the children may have taken——"

"Mother questioned the children," he intervened quickly.

"They are afraid of her."

His face went white. "Don't say that!"

"Is it not true?"

"Oh, Katharine," he pleaded. "Be sensible. Say that you took the brooch and get out."

"You are afraid of her, too," she accused, at once pitying and despising him. "Do *you* think me a thief?"

"I—I don't know. The brooch was found in your room, and Mattie swears she saw you in Mother's chamber just before the loss was discovered. What am I to think?" he asked wretchedly. "Who could blame you? You have only your wages—no family, no future—" He broke off before the scorn in her eyes.

"I am not a thief," she repeated coldly, turning her back on him.

The coach swayed sharply, and Katharine came back to the present. They were well into London now, she saw in swift shock, a London, until today, as beloved as it was familiar. To her right she recognized Hyde Park, its gaunt trees icy from the freezing rain. Here in the western section of the city, handsome brick houses lined the squares and streets. Her own early home had been one much like the dwelling they were now passing. A sedan chair, servants in yellow livery shivering beside it, stood before a gracious doorway, and she watched a girl no older than herself descend the sanded steps, a lavender-gloved hand upon the rail, the white plumes of her turban tossing to and fro. As she moved, beneath her dark cloak her gray gown of iridescent silk reflected the light like a dove's wing. Katharine glanced down at her own gray dress, and her lips twitched in a bitter smile. We are like two birds, she thought, observing the girl being helped into the chair, but I am caged and she is free.

As they rumbled along Oxford Street, she continued to stare out of the window, trying to catch and store up in her memory everything that met her eyes. A taste of the county jail had taught her how interminable the days and nights of prison life could be. Now, looking out across the road into Soho Square, she saw an old woman hobble across the cobblestones, and suddenly stumbling, put out a frantic hand to grasp the palings guarding the statue of King Charles II. Katharine watched her slowly regain her balance, look up to the statue as if it were a deity, and then bob in quick obeisance.

Beside her Michael Edes laughed in quiet amusement. "Surely His late Majesty cannot appreciate such homage now," he murmured. With a grateful smile the girl turned to him, more than ever thankful for his presence as they moved deeper and deeper into the heart of the city.

In Holbourn Street traffic thickened, and the coach rolled more slowly over the bumpy pavement, groaning as the wheels struck the uneven stones. Here, despite the bitter cold, a few wretches hawked their wares.

"Buy my pincushions—my pretty pincushions!" A young woman put up chilblained fingers as red as her wares against the window, and Michael Edes let down the glass to give her a coin. He was less charitable, however, to a ragged beggar who ran alongside, thrusting up a huge rattrap made of wire ingeniously twisted into a cage. Katharine, reminded of her own fate, shuddered at the contraption. Seeing her blanched face, the doctor struck the pedlar's hand from the coach with an angry oath and banged the window shut.

They crossed Holbourn Bridge and continued relentlessly onward. Shrinking deeper into the cloak, Katharine closed her eyes, trying to shut out the familiar landmarks, wishing they would disappear and that she would find herself, when the coach stopped, in some new and distant place, miraculously removed from the King's justice. She raised her face at last to find her companion's grave eyes upon her.

"I fear there is no refuge," he said gently.

She made no answer, for now, in the shadow of the prison, a slow terror began to wash over her like a chill tide, numbing her heart and drowning her speech. As they passed through a gate into the prison yard, she noticed a stone figure adorning a niche in the wall, the word *Libertas* inscribed on her cap. Her own freedom, the girl reflected in grim irony, she herself had sacrificed to truth—and injured pride.

The coach stopped, the step was lowered, and Michael Edes sprang down to help her alight. Silently she drew off the gloves and gave them to him. And now, looking up, she saw fully the great gray prison and felt the weight of its immensity press down on her like a block of stone. She began to tremble and clung to the man at her side.

"I do not know your sentence," he said in a low voice. "Are you to be transported?"

Katharine shook her head. The judge's words, harsh and final, seemed even now unreal. "I—I am sentenced to fourteen years," she whispered.

"In the eyes of his Lordship, a merciful sentence, no doubt, for a thief."

Deaf to his sardonic tone, she heard only the last cruel word and winced.

"I ask your pardon! God knows I did not mean to accuse you!" Catching up her hands, he pressed them to his lips. Then, releasing them, he fumbled in the pocket of his riding coat. "Take these," he said earnestly. She felt coins pressed between her fingers. "And keep the cloak, I beg. You may have need of it."

"Thank you."

Withdrawing from him, Katharine turned away, striving desperately for some semblance of dignity as she shuffled after the guard, the chain rattling over the stones of the yard. She moved in a kind of dream, unable even now to believe the nightmare real.

In a small lodge at the prison entrance where all new-comers were received, the formalities of becoming a ward of Newgate were quickly completed. As entrance fee, the sum of two shillings, sixpence was demanded, and Katharine reluctantly paid the coins into the grasping hands of a turnkey, who also secured into his own keeping the silver-handled scissors from her sewing kit as well as her gold thimble. Then he led her, still shackled, to the foot of a stone staircase. To her surprise he assisted her up the stairs, a gallantry at once obliterated by his coarse fondling of her hair.

"Rainin' much?" His thick fingers had entangled themselves in her curls.

"No," she whispered, shrinking away from him. "Not —not now."

"What ye in for?"

"Stealing."

He shrugged and transferred his hand to the shoulder capes of the riding cloak the doctor had given her, appraising it with the touch of an expert.

"Ye'll have to pay to keep it."

"The—the cloak?"

He nodded. "The others'll want it."

They had reached the second floor, and here the stench of sweat, dampness, and gin, mixed with the oily smudge that rose from the wall burners, was sickening. Beneath a flaring wall torch Katharine stumbled to a halt.

"I feel faint," she faltered.

"Ye'll get used to it." But he allowed her a moment to lean against the stone wall, whose dripping dampness penetrated even the thick folds of her cloak.

"Come along now." His hand closed on her arm.

In the room they entered next, an anvil was set up. Beside it sat a man, idly smoking.

The turnkey gave Katharine a shrewd glance. "Ye want yer irons off?"

"If you please."

"Ye'll have to pay easement money." His eyes narrowed as they moved over her. "How much will ye give?"

Katharine studied him. She had been wrong, she

realized, in her first judgment of him. It was not she herself that whetted his interest. It was the money he could wring from her. The scissors and thimble he had pilfered would fetch a good price. Now he demanded more. Was the man insatiable?

"What is your usual fee?" she asked slowly.

He laughed, showing tobacco-stained teeth in a narrow mouth. "It depends. To you"—his eyes assessed her again, touching the cloak and bonnet—"easement ought to be worth a guinea."

"A guinea!" she gasped. "That's extortion!"

Again he laughed and shrugged.

"Pay it," the man at the anvil said softly.

Turning her back on them both, she searched her purse, extracting one of the coins Michael Edes had given her.

With a grin the turnkey pocketed the coin. "We'll git all ye have before long," he boasted.

Striking off the shackles was no easy task, and Katharine was exhausted when at last she was free of them. Deeply grateful to the smith, she thanked him.

"Steer clear o' Goss when ye can," the man muttered, putting down his hammer and punch and casting a sidelong glance at the turnkey. "He's a mean one."

Even before they came to the felons' ward, the noise from it deafened her. When they entered, Katharine fell back a pace, appalled at the sight. Some thirty women were strewn like ninepins across the narrow room. A few slept on cots; others, dull-eyed and dirty, stood listlessly against the walls; some, she saw in horror, still wore irons on their hands and feet. On the floor, in the center of the room, a large group in wild disarray played cards.

"Here ye be. Ye'll find a place over there." With a wave of his hand toward the far corner, Goss took his leave.

No sooner was he gone than the cardplayers flung down their cards and with derisive mutterings approached her.

"A lady!" Spitting on her forefinger, one ran it along Katharine's cheek. "Clean and respectable!" she jeered.

Another snatched the ribbon from her hair. " 'Igh and mighty!"

"What's she done to deserve such a cloak, I'd like to know?"

"What ain't she done, dearie!"

"Shut up, all of you." A tall, bony woman took command. "Now then, my pretty." She eyed Katharine boldly. "Pay or strip!"

"Chummage! Chummage!" The voices rose in chorus.

This demand was the time-honored custom in London prisons. The new prisoner either paid for the privilege of keeping her clothing, or all but a few garments were stripped from her back.

"Toe to top. We'll begin with her feet." The tall woman who had silenced them raised Katharine's skirts and studied her muddy shoes. "Worth a shilling, chums?"

"Two!"

"Two it is. Stockings?"

They thronged round, peering at Katharine's stockings, stained and torn.

"Let 'er keep 'em." A pale, emaciated girl spoke in disgust. "They ain't no better than ours."

"Petticoat?"

The dirty hem of her petticoat was viewed judicially.

"Three shillings!" a voice called.

"Gown?"

Katharine tried to stand motionless while several prisoners ran their stubby fingers over her gown. Soiled as it was, she saw now that the dress was regal compared with the rags covering most of the women. But the dress did not meet with approval.

"No lace anywhere."

"And no ribbons."

"Not very generous—whoever gave it her."

"Why couldn't it be red or green?"

"Ten shillings?" the auctioneer suggested.

"Aye," they agreed.

She was allowed to keep the bonnet and shawl for a small sum. Most of the women wore shawls, she noticed, and a bonnet in prison was an incongruous addition to one's wardrobe.

"And now the cloak." The bony hand flung open the

cloak to its full circle. "Three capes!" she announced
with relish, ruffling the shoulder capes.

The cloak would be her only protection against the
raw dampness of the place, summer or winter, Katharine knew. Others knew it, too, she saw from the calculating eyes that confronted her. The cloak would
come high.

"A pound!"

"More!"

"A guinea!"

"Two guineas!"

Within the warmth of the cloak, Katharine shivered,
trying to recall the exact coins Michael Edes had given
her.

The women were suddenly silent, and she realized
the ordeal was over.

"Three guineas will cover everything nicely, my
pretty." The woman stretched out her hand. "Ye can
keep all ye've got on, and we'll celebrate yer comin' in
yer own coin," she said with a taunting laugh.

From her pocket Katharine pulled her purse, trying
to keep its contents hidden from the curious, probing
eyes that surrounded her. Slowly she counted out three
guineas. Her outrage at the barbarous custom was lost
in overwhelming gratitude to the man who had been
so generous to her. How little he had said, yet how
much he must have known of the indignities that
awaited her here.

There was a shout as the coins were tossed into the air, and three of the women caught them.

Slowly Katharine made her way to her cot. One side was hard against the stone wall, cold and clammy to her touch. The side on which she had room to stand was separated by no more than eighteen inches from another bed on which lay a thin-faced, hollow-eyed girl only a year or two older than herself. Within the circle of her arms she held a sleeping child.

"I'm afraid he may cry when he wakes," the girl apologized. "If ye want to sleep, it had best be now."

"I'm not sleepy," Katharine replied in a low voice so as not to wake the child. "And please don't fret. Children have to cry sometime," she added with a smile.

"He's so hungry. There's never enough food to go round." It was not plaintive, merely matter-of-fact.

"I understand."

The girl sighed as she looked at her new neighbor. "Ye—ye look so clean and pretty."

"Thank you. There was soap and water at the last inn."

"There's water to be had here, but no towels. Ye'll have to use yer petticoat." She hitched herself up on one shoulder in order to make the next point. "And ye'll have to fight for yer food. That's why Billy and me is so hungry all the time. We can't get there fast enough when they dole it out." She lay back, and Katharine saw beneath the threadbare blanket the irons that chained her ankles.

"I know," she murmured again, hardly realizing what she said, yet longing to be of comfort. And then suddenly she was unable to stand upright another moment, and sinking down on the cot she stretched out and closed her eyes.

I cannot bear this, she thought in anguish. The women, callous, filthy, raucous, she had anticipated. But the child—rumpled, pink-cheeked in sleep, so close she could reach out and touch him—this was an unexpected torment. What had she done, what *could* she have done, this sad-eyed mother, to be so punished in this grisly place? Katharine turned to the wall, hiding her face in her hands. But although she could shroud the misery before her eyes, she could not muffle the noise in her ears, now growing louder each moment.

"They're drinkin' up yer money," the older girl said in resignation. "Ye'll get no sleep now."

Her companion made no answer. The narrow, hard bed took her back to her childhood. Just such a bed had stood in the chamber of her aunt's house, when, as an orphaned ten-year-old, Katharine had come to claim it, weeping out her grief and loneliness beneath a hemstitched coverlet.

Her aunt was a stern realist, she had learned at breakfast the next morning as they sat together overlooking the countryside through the windows of the breakfast parlor.

"Your father's madness—and gambling *is* a madness —killed your mother," her relative told her bluntly.

"Now he is gone, too, and you are penniless." Fastening her gaze on the trembling girl, she had scrutinized her ruthlessly. "Your face is too thin ever to be really beautiful, I fear, though your eyes are good—that dark, sea-blue color comes from your mother's side. And you have the Randolph hair." Reaching out, she touched a strand of Katharine's hair. "Mine was like this—black as a raven's wing, thick and heavy." She gave a long sigh. "If you were a great beauty, we could pin our hopes on a good marriage. But you are not, and I fear you never will be." Turning back to the plate before her, she chipped the shell from her egg and plunged a finger of bread into it. Then she looked hard at her niece again. "Women who have neither face nor fortune must live by their wits," she said with candor. "There's no road open to you but teaching, more's the pity."

There had been Mr. Percy, the dancing master; Miss Avery, the governess; Mademoiselle for French; old Mrs. Hibbard for sewing and embroidery; Miss Beveridge for music and drawing. For six long years, the girl recalled grimly, lessons had been thrust upon her wherever her aunt was in residence, country or town. But her own determination to prove herself, to wrench one word of praise from her unyielding old relative, had finally borne fruit.

"You are better prepared than most governesses," her aunt had conceded a little before her niece's sixteenth birthday. "And it is just as well, for you must begin at once." She interrupted herself with a harsh cough that set the black ribbons on her cap trembling, and Katharine saw with misgivings how old and ill she had become. "When I am gone, there will be nothing left," she continued in harsh tones. "I have lived on credit too long." Then, in the only display of affection she had ever indulged in, she drew Katharine within the compass of her arms. "You have done well, child. You have backbone and grit. And in the long run they will stand you in better stead than a beautiful face or a handsome fortune."

In another two months her aunt was dead, the property in the hands of creditors as she had predicted, and Katharine, through the offices of a family friend who had since died, was applying for a position with Lady Blaize, a recent widow with three young daughters who required the services of a governess.

"How old are you?" Even now Lady Blaize's imperious voice cut through her memory like a scythe.

"Eighteen, your ladyship." It had been her only falsehood.

The flabby hand, hard with jewels, lifted the lorgnette, and the older woman examined her with deliberation. Katharine felt a prick of terror. For the eyes upon her were cold, dispassionate, as if they regarded a marble statue offered for sale—a statue that could be purchased cheaply, placed indifferently as chance dictated, or discarded at the owner's whim.

"You have all the qualifications but experience. Can you begin at once?"

"Yes, your ladyship."

The next day she had commenced to teach the little girls, docile, obedient creatures, pathetically responsive to praise and affection. The youngest child, Charles, a boy of four and his mother's darling, was still in the charge of an old nurse. Lacking the discipline of a father and indulged by a doting mother, this son was spoiled beyond measure and given the run of the great old house.

Several weeks had elapsed before the young lord and heir made an appearance. Then, late one morning when Katharine and the girls were walking along the immaculate paths of the gardens, Lord Blaize, magnificent in the silks and laces of a London blade, appeared. In surprise and excitement his sisters threw themselves upon him.

"Quarter! Quarter, I beg! Show me some mercy!" he protested with a laugh, disentangling himself from their embraces. His eyes, quick and bold, met Katharine's, and there was pleasure in his glance, and interest.

He swept her a bow. "Your most obedient servant, ma'am."

"My lord," she murmured, going down in a curtsy.

"It's Miss Leslie, our new governess," Jane, the eldest, explained. "She's the kindest Mamma has ever found for us—and the fairest!" she finished earnestly, with a warm glance at her teacher.

"Certainly the fairest," he murmured, and seeing Katharine's color rise at this flattering interpretation of the word, he was quick to press his advantage. "Of that there can be not the slightest doubt."

In the four months they had known each other, he had employed no stratagems—he had simply pursued her. Had she been older, experienced ever so little in the ways of the world, would she have recognized his advances for what they were—the extravagant compliments of a skilled philanderer? But she did not want to recognize them as such, she knew now. Here was a ready answer to her dream. Happily she treasured each tender word, seeing herself cherished and secure, mistress eventually of Blaize House and all its munificent bounty.

She was not so naive as to suppose that marriage between them would come easily. After all, she was merely a governess. But her family was of old and honorable lineage, and although her father's weakness had brought financial ruin, no lasting stigma attached to the name —every debt had been paid. What Katharine did not consider were Lady Blaize's lofty ambitions for her elder son. With mounting concern her ladyship had witnessed his increasing devotion, and whereas the casual dalliance of a young lord with his sisters' governess might be laughed away, the possibility of marriage could not be. The discovery of the brooch in Katharine's room, following the disappearance of a valuable necklace two weeks earlier, had given her ladyship a convincing weapon. Although Jay had not openly branded her a thief, he had doubted her integrity, and these doubts had strengthened Katharine's resolve to fight for her name. Lady Blaize had taken her stubborn refusal to admit to the theft as a personal challenge, and had angrily carried out her threat to bring charges. Her son had thought Katharine a fool. Neither one had acknowledged that the girl's survival, both professional and personal, hung on her honor, her good name.

Now she turned the matter over again in her mind. Who had thrust the emerald brooch deep into the toe of one of her dancing slippers, and then hidden the slipper in the darkest corner of her closet? Why had Mattie sworn she had seen Katharine in Lady Blaize's chamber—a room she had never entered in her life? She could find no answers to these questions then, and none now, as she twisted and turned on the prison cot.

Beside her the child began to whimper, and Katharine heard the gentle words of the girl as she tried to comfort him. She opened her eyes to the narrow, barred windows set high in the stone wall, to the flaring, grotesque shadows cast by the oil links, to the irresolute prisoners strewn across the room. Now, for the first time, she saw fully her own plight, and the judge's words repeated themselves in her mind.

"For malicious and premeditated theft, I sentence you, Katharine Leslie, to fourteen years' imprisonment."

The nightmare was in truth a reality, and overwhelmed by its intensity, Katharine wept.

The days that followed fell into a pattern of dull monotony unrelieved in the ward except for occasional quarrels that sprang up swift and fierce as summer storms and as quickly abated. Prisoners were led out regularly, though rarely to freedom, Katharine discovered. Most of the women were sent aboard the King's ships to be transported overseas to one of the several British colonies in the West Indies—Antigua, Barbados, Jamaica.

This was the fate awaiting Mary Fletcher and the child Billy, she learned one April morning.

"We'll be goin' aboard someday before too long, I'm thinkin'." Mary smoothed Billy's rumpled hair with a motherly hand. "They can't crowd many more in here!"

Katharine made no reply. She had heard of the transports—old, dark, and below decks a chill damp never touched by the sun—these ships were the worst prisons of all, with their foul water, stale food, and constant, sickening motion. But at the end of the voyage, if the convict survived, there was a chance of life in a new land.

"What of your husband, Mary?" she asked now.

"Who knows where he's got to?" Mary spread her hands wide. "He never would have let Billy and me starve, ye can count on that," she said defensively. "If he'd been able to reach us, I wouldn't have had to steal to keep body and soul together. No," she went on, "if ye ask me, some press gang fell on him and tossed him aboard a King's vessel. Who'd serve in one of them rotten ships unless he was forced to? Maybe he'll desert," she finished darkly.

Katharine said nothing. Mary's ethics and outlook were very different from her own, she had come to realize. Six months ago such a tough-minded philosophy as her friend professed would have shocked her. But Mary was a child of the streets in a city of thieves and cutthroats as well as of lords and ladies. She had battled for her own existence; she had stolen for Billy's. Her language and point of view might not be those of a gentlewoman, the girl reflected, yet compared with

Lady Blaize, Mary had the fine, strong-fibered strength
of new linen tested against rotting silk.

Katharine tried another subject on which they had
talked before.

"If you go aboard ship, you'll be badly hampered by
those leg irons," she said in firm tones. "You must let
me help you, Mary! The smith can strike them off in
no time."

The older girl's eyes grew warm and she smiled. But
she shook her head decisively. "Ye'll need yer money,
believe me, every penny of it." With a gentle hand she
touched Katharine's arm in a gesture of gratitude. "I've
taken yer ointment for Billy's rash, haven't I? And it's
helped a good bit, don't ye think?" she asked eagerly.

Katharine nodded. The ointment Michael Edes had
given her seemed to relieve the terrible itch that covered Billy's emaciated little body. Hot water and soap,
she suspected, would have done even more. The boy
abandoned his mother's lap now, and climbed into
Katharine's. If only there were some way of keeping
him clean, she thought in despair, as she touched his
cheek with a caressing hand.

"And I'm not forgettin' how ye fight for our food,"
Mary added grimly.

"My own, too, remember!" The younger girl gave a
little laugh. "And I enjoy it." The cold selfishness of the
women of the ward so angered her that she took sav-
age pleasure in elbowing her way into the melee each
noon to fight tooth and nail for the full share of bread

and meat scraps rightfully belonging to the three of them.

"As long as ye are here, ye'll have to go on payin' for a bed, just as we all do now. And next winter, same as this, it'll cost ye to go near the fire. An extra blanket will cost, so will a candle." Mary shook her head again. "No, ye can't afford to be generous."

"You can't afford to wear those leg irons much longer either!" Katharine protested hotly. "What is it now—four months?" she asked harshly, looking at one of Mary's ankles where a chafing iron had caused a sore that never seemed to heal. "Who will mind Billy, if—if anything happens to you?"

This was a cruel thrust, but she made it deliberately. Any day infection might set in and send Mary into a raging fever. The shackles had to come off. Just as she never accepted anything for herself, so her neighbor never yet had refused anything for her child. Katharine saw her eyes on Billy now as Mary struggled with her pride.

"As ye will," she said at last.

Billy between them, they sought out the turnkey and the smith.

"How much will ye pay?" Goss demanded.

Mary gave him a scornful look. "Ye well know ye've taken all I have!" she said bitingly. "I've nothin' left!"

He grinned knowingly at Katharine. "But yer friend has."

She was silent, and for a long moment each appraised the other.

"A crown," the jailer demanded.

"Thief!" Mary spat out the word.

With a shrug he turned to Katharine. "A crown it is. Pay up."

She dropped the coin into his hand and he took it with a tantalizing laugh. "Remember? I told ye we'd have it all before long. But I didn't expect ye to be fool enough to spend it on someone else," he added contemptuously.

When he had gone, the smith set to work. As he tried to move the irons into a position where he could strike them off more easily, Mary groaned with the pain.

"Ye're not gettin' 'em off any too soon," the man grumbled. But there was a note of compassion in his voice. A prisoner like themselves, he was assigned this task. He saw none of the easement money, though it was his deftness that relieved the agonies of the shackled.

That afternoon a turnkey informed Mary that a friend awaited her in the hall below.

Mary sighed. "I haven't got the money to see me down," she said in resignation, referring to the fee demanded of prisoners before they could enter the visitors' hall.

"I'll see you down." Before Mary could protest, Katharine gave the man a sixpence.

"A candle to light her down will cost another penny," he reminded her.

She gave him the penny.

"If she pays, she should be able to come, too," Mary said belligerently.

Goss would have mocked such a suggestion, Katharine thought, but this man merely shrugged. "Go along, all three of ye," he said indifferently. "What's it to me?"

A few minutes later Mary greeted a small woman swathed in a black fringed shawl. "This is my friend, Annie Moore," she explained to Katharine. "She's a maid at The Bell in Warwick Street."

While the two friends chatted together, Katharine led Billy around the hall, a dimly lit, large room filled with prisoners and visitors seated on wooden benches along the walls. When she had circled the room once, Mary beckoned her to join them.

"Annie knows some of the doctors from the College, she says. The tavern she works in is close by. What's yer friend's name?"

"Michael Edes." Katharine blushed. She had told Mary of the young doctor's generosity, but she was not prepared to share the experience with a stranger. "I—I scarcely know him," she protested.

"They often come in for a mug o' ale," Annie explained casually. "Maybe someday I'll see him. Oh, I almost forgot!" Fumbling in her pocket, she brought up a small gingerbread and gave it to Billy, who munched it happily all the way back to the ward.

Katharine had early discovered that within the walls the prisoners enjoyed a surprising amount of freedom. Every day men and women felons could be seen chatting in small groups, often gambling at cards. The taproom sold gin and tobacco to the wretches who could afford it. Occasionally debtors and their wives and families appeared on the felons' side of the prison. The parents were miserable enough, but the children, their small faces pinched and peaked, looked as old as their fathers. Billy stared at them when they appeared, and they stared back with the dull, opaque eyes of the ever-hungry and ill.

On all three floors there were spacious single rooms with heat and light and air. These, she learned from Mary one day as they walked about with Billy, were rented to wealthy felons who, through the generosity of friends or their own contriving, could afford such luxurious quarters. Now the door of one room was thrown open, and a handsome man, dressed in the height of fashion—silk breeches, brocade coat, ruffles at the wrist, and huge silver buckles on his shoes—confronted them.

"Welcome, my dears." He swept them an exaggerated bow.

Katharine drew back sharply, but Mary laughed.

"Oh, we're not payin' a call, sir," she said airily. "Just passin' by."

"You disappoint me." His eyes, black and bold, were on Katharine.

"Up to yer old tricks and caught at it this time, I'll wager," Mary challenged.

"Alas, yes." With an easy grace he leaned against the doorway. "But I have been caught before."

"Maybe ye'll not be so lucky gettin' away this time."

"Who knows?" With a flick of the wrist he opened a tortoise-shell case, took a pinch of snuff, and sneezed into an immaculate handkerchief. Katharine watched him in fascination. Looking up, he met her eyes and smiled, though he still spoke to Mary. "Will you be my guests at a party I am having on Wednesday next? All the *ton*, ladies and gentlemen of the highest fashion, need I add, are planning to attend."

Mary took the cards he offered. "Thank you, but we make no promises," she said a little tartly. Turning Billy about, they retraced their steps, the child peering after the stranger and following with lagging steps.

"Who is he?" Katharine asked.

"Jack Winston, the highwayman." With a curious expression in her eyes, Mary looked at her friend. "Ye must have heard of him surely? All London knows Jack. At least all my part of London," she added wryly.

"I've heard of him," the younger girl admitted.

"He robbed one of the King's friends. This time they'll hang him for sure." There was real regret in

Mary's voice. "He's given away a fortune to the poor, even if the money was stolen," she added aggressively.

Katharine offered no argument. Mary, she knew, was in sympathy with men such as Jack Winston. That they robbed the rich to indulge the poor made them no less thieves. But in Mary's eyes the handful of coins tossed by a debonair thief to a London beggar justified the initial crime.

Now, back in the ward, Katharine found the atmosphere insufferable. It was the idleness of prison life that was so frustrating, she thought hopelessly. No wonder the card games assumed such importance! There were no books to read; there was no handwork provided. If only there were a scrap of material, she could sew. Mary's homespun gown was threadbare. Billy was in rags. The small boy had crawled onto the cot and lay there, half-naked, listlessly sucking his thumb.

In a gesture of desperation she thrust her own hands deep into the pockets of her gown. Though the purse that touched her fingers now held only one or two coins, she did not regret what she had spent on Mary. In her other pocket her fingers met her small sewing kit, then, below it, she felt the soft leather covers of her Psalter. A flush of shame burned her cheeks. Anger and frustration had so consumed her in this hateful place that she had not once opened the covers, she thought with remorse.

Now, as she withdrew the book, she found Mary's eyes upon her. "Would you like to read, Mary?" Katharine offered the Psalter to her companion, who took the slender volume gingerly, turned the pages with a bemused look, and then returned it.

"I—I never learned to read."

Mary's illiteracy was not unusual, yet as she acknowledged it, Katharine was swept with a flood of guilt. All of the teachers she herself had studied under, all of the lessons she had taken so for granted—had she deserved them any more than Mary? Because Fortune had smiled upon her, she could read and write. Because her aunt had offered her further instruction, she had developed other skills. Money! *Money!* she thought in angry helplessness. Money paved the road to comfort and security. As little as her aunt possessed bought learning. As much as Lady Blaize commanded bought power. Even here in prison it was gold that obtained the smallest comforts —the shabby gown that covered one's nakedness, the shackles struck off, the pillow or blanket, the stubby candle. Enough gold could purchase the luxuries that highwayman Jack Winston reveled in—clean linen, choice food, fresh air. *Money!* If ever she got out, she'd contrive never to be poor again!

Mary's cool, dispassionate acceptance of her fate roused her to deeper anger. To read and to write— these were such simple joys. Why should Mary be denied them? Lack of time might have answered once; it did no longer. With this thought she swung round on Mary, her eyes bright with challenge.

"You may never have had the time or opportunity

to learn, Mary. Well,"—her voice sharpened—"there's time enough now!"

"Ye mean—ye'll teach me?"

"Oh, Mary, of course I'll teach you!" Katharine threw herself down on the cot beside her friend. "And we'll begin now—this very minute. Do you know any of your letters?"

"Some," Mary answered cautiously.

As Katharine picked up the Psalter again, it fell open, and her eyes ran over the opening words of the One Hundred and Twenty-first Psalm.

> *I will lift up mine eyes unto the hills; from*
> *whence cometh my help?*
> *My help cometh even from the Lord, who*
> *hath made heaven and earth.*

This had been her aunt's favorite psalm, and as she read the words aloud, familiar and beautiful, the old woman came vividly to mind. Hers had been a simple faith, a belief founded firmly on the value of personal effort, the girl reflected, recalling her relative's constant admonition: "God helps those who help themselves." Why had she forgotten? Why had she despaired in this place? She would fight, and her first battle would be for Mary—the Psalter her weapon.

Looking at Mary, Katharine experienced the same trembling shock of excitement that had engulfed her the first morning she had begun to teach the Blaize children. And Mary, she saw with a rush of affectionate compassion, looked as apprehensive as a small child.

"Tell me the name of the letter I point to," she said gently, putting her finger beneath a word of the psalm and beginning their first lesson.

Mary proved a diligent pupil. She labored from the moment the pale light crept through the prison windows until the torches cast shadows so deep that neither she nor her teacher could make out the words.

"If only we had candles!" Katharine sighed one rainy evening when the darkness descended earlier than usual. But she dared not risk her few remaining pennies on such a luxury.

Billy seemed content to do little other than to walk briefly each day with his mother and her friend in the room given over to exercise. Katharine was disturbed by his apathy. He made almost no attempt to speak, and surely a child nearly two should demand more activity! She could only suppose the wretched food and lack of fresh air were responsible for his lethargy.

After Tuesday's allotment of moldy bread and cold tea, Mary drew Katharine aside.

"Tomorrow is Jack Winston's party. Are ye plannin' to go?"

"No." Though she had not succeeded in forgetting the dashing thief, she had no intention of continuing the acquaintance.

"Ye're makin' a mistake." Deftly Mary spread the

ragged blanket over Billy's spindly legs as he slept. "The company may not be the best, to be sure, but the food'll be worth it."

"What do you mean?"

"There'll be roast ducklin', boiled fowl, pies and tarts —every London pieman will be there, I'm guessin'— cakes and wine, fruit——"

"Mary!" Katharine interrupted, her eyes wide and her mouth beginning to water.

Mary laughed at her expression. "I'll be keepin' an eye on Billy here. But there's no need for anyone else to. If ye go, we could all feast on the fat o' the land." From under her mattress, softly, so as not to disturb the sleeping child, Mary drew out a flour sack. "This holds a good bit," she confided.

Katharine stared. To accept the hospitality of Jack Winston and then to steal his food—it was like an invited guest slipping the silver spoons into his pocket.

I can't do it, she thought. But the words in her mind did not reach her lips. Hunger today was so deep and raw in all of them that she knew, if the chance came, she could and would steal for Billy, for Mary, for herself.

"Highwayman or not, ye're goin' to need a friend when Billy and me's gone." Mary looked hard at her. "Ye've not heard from the doctor?"

"No." Expectant, hoping for she knew not what, Katharine had spent the early days and nights dreaming of Michael Edes. But as the weeks and months crept by with no message and no sign of him, she had begun to doubt his interest. Perhaps, after all, the generous gift of money had been his way of saying farewell.

"If I do go to the party—mind, I have not said I shall," she said slowly, aware that her forces were crumbling; "what would I wear?"

With a leisurely candor Mary scrutinized her, and under her critical eye Katharine became painfully conscious of her appearance. Though they showed only when she walked, the stockings she had washed with such care had not yielded up their stains. Limp and bedraggled, the gray gown hung from a figure now refined almost to gauntness by prison fare. And her kid slippers had never recovered from the mud of the innyard.

"I look like a scarecrow," she whispered.

"Ye can wash yer face and hands, can't ye?"

"Yes."

"And ye can wear the cloak. Other guests will be in shawls and cloaks, especially if it's rainin'."

Rain, Katharine mused, rain—falling across the fields, cool and wet on the grass—it had been weeks now since she had felt the rain. And the sun—once she had known the sun—bright, hot to her skin, warming her whole being with its splendor. Could she wait months and years without the touch of either? Surely there was some way out of this loathsome place. Soon Mary and Billy would escape it—granted a slim chance for life in another land, while the girl she now was would vanish with the years, becoming one of the sad wretches she pitied so deeply—passive and uncaring.

Rain, perhaps sun, and *food*—the thought was exhilarating. Katharine faced her friend. "I'll go," she said firmly, taking up the bag and thrusting it beneath her own mattress.

Since his guests were too numerous to be accommodated in his rooms, Jack Winston had hired the yard, Katharine discovered the next day when she showed her admission card to a turnkey. She was guided down the stone steps to the first floor and out into the enclosure given over to wealthy prisoners for relaxation and exercise. Fresh and cool, the spring air struck her lungs like wind from the sea, and she gulped in great breaths of it. Then, as the tangy fragrance of roast duck tickled her nostrils, her hand clutched the bag secured beneath her cloak. Tender duckling for Mary, she decided, boiled chicken or fowl for Billy, and as many sweets as she could tuck away.

Already many guests had gathered near two large tables. Gentlemen, richly garbed in silk breeches and brocade coats, chatted together, while ladies swished about in soft satins and flowered muslins, their heads swathed in modish turbans, their hands covered in gloves of every pastel shade. I must hide my hands, Katharine thought in panic, for no lady ever appeared in public without gloves. But she was no longer a lady,

she recalled ruefully. She had come neither to be admired nor to flatter, but to steal.

"You are in good time." Her host was suddenly at
her side, and Katharine dipped in a curtsy.

He gave a look around. "Are you alone?"

"Yes, sir."

"I am flattered that you came at all," he said with a
light laugh. "I did not suppose at our last meeting that
your companion regarded me as—as quite the most
fitting host for the young."

"No," Katharine admitted with a smile, recalling
Mary's final admonitions, "I fear she does not."

"Then why, pray, are you here?" The black eyes were
a challenge.

"Because I am hungry," she admitted with candor.

He laughed heartily, and his glance touching her now
was one of amusement. "I am well set down and by a
schoolgirl at that! Not another lady here would admit
to hunger. *I* am supposed to be the attraction."

Katharine looked up at him. Coupled with a hard
and handsome face, a lithe and exquisitely groomed
figure, he possessed a wit and humor that intensified his
charm. There would be many London ladies, she knew,
who would find him irresistible, not the less so because
in a few weeks he would probably hang for his crimes.
Now, like a bear in a cage, he was a curiosity, something
to see, someone to talk about. And like a clever animal
he acted the part he himself had chosen to play. Seeing
him in a keener light, she felt a swift pity.

"It seems such a waste," she murmured.

He was quick to understand her. "My life?"

"Yes."

"If it has been, I shall be the last to admit it."

"Perhaps—perhaps you can escape again?"

He gave a curt laugh. "I bought my way out last time. I fear it won't work again."

Taking her arm, he led her to a table, and she found herself amid the fragrant perfumes of the ladies and the more delectable odors of the food.

"Choose what you wish," he said carelessly and left her.

She watched a pieman, his tray of pies balanced easily on one hand, set his wares upon a table and then hurry off to his street stall to secure more. Then her attention riveted upon the food. Wines, cheeses, puddings, a breast of veal, a roast goose—the array was bewildering. A slice of chicken was so tender it seemed to melt on her tongue. The duckling was rich and succulent. And the small cakes topped with frosting were delicious. Mary and Billy must have all these and any other delicacies she could garner.

But to secure them was not easy. Since she was obviously not one of them, the ladies stared at her, their eyes hard and shrewd, while the gentlemen watched her in cool detachment through their quizzing glasses. Casually she nibbled, trying to appear unconcerned. But to her dismay, her own appetite, so ravenous when she had first arrived, diminished rapidly as her nervousness mounted.

Stubbornly she moved closer to the table. She had come here for food and she would have it! Selecting a chicken leg, she pretended to gnaw at it, then moved her hand to the opening of her cloak and thrust it quickly within. No one appeared to notice, and she approached the sliced veal.

"May I recommend the goose, ma'am?" One of the gentlemen addressed her and Katharine started. Beneath small, sly eyes, his face hung fat and heavy, and he smiled ingratiatingly.

"No—no, I thank you." She moved hastily away from him.

"Nor the roast lamb?" Again he was beside her.

"I—I thank you, no."

"Perhaps the lamb's tongues?"

Across the table now she saw the ladies laughing behind their fans, while the gentlemen regarded her with amused, ironic eyes. This, then, was a game in which she was the badger and the fat gentleman the hound. But she could not afford to play games, Katharine thought angrily—unless she made the rules. Perhaps she could make it worth her while, and looking up into the heavy face so close to her own, she gave a flirtatious smile. At the same moment she thrust out her foot and her pursuer tripped against it, striking the table hard. As he did so Katharine jerked the cloth, and pies, cheeses, roasts, and wine crashed to the ground amid the shrieks of the ladies and the oaths of the men. Waiters raced to rescue the dishes and place them again on the table. Katharine, too, dipped down, but what she gleaned went instantly into the flour sack beneath her cloak. When she rose she found Jack Winston beside her, his keen eyes hard on hers.

"Such a catastrophe!" he said dryly. "You are certain you have recovered—everything?"

Her face grew red, and she looked away in confusion. With a laugh he drew her aside, beyond the stares of the other guests.

"Have you had enough to eat?" he asked seriously.

She nodded, too abashed to speak.

"Then I think you had better go. Your friend was quite justified in her fears. This party is no place for you. But neither is Newgate." He looked at her curiously. "How the devil did you get here?"

"I—I was convicted of stealing."

"We are birds of the same feather. But you, I'll wager, are innocent. Any competent thief would die of shame to be caught lifting food with the awkward manners you employ!"

"I beg your pardon," she murmured wretchedly. "I wanted something to—to take back——"

"I have provided for that. I have sent a turnkey to ask your friends to come here, so they can share some of the feast with you."

They moved now to the end of the yard where an opening led back within the prison walls.

"Have you no one who can help you?" he asked earnestly, looking down at her. "No one with money?"

"No."

He was silent, his fingers playing with the handsome snuffbox. "A few more months here and you will have neither the energy nor the wit with which to think and plan. If I could help—but I have very little left, and it must go to those I am indebted to."

"I do not expect your help," Katharine said, astonished. Then, touched by his concern, she spoke more gently. "What about yourself?"

"I have no excuse. I gambled a fortune away. I chose the life I lead." He shrugged. "If I hang, I'll get no less than I deserve, perhaps."

As they came to the stairway, he put a hand on her arm, and she drew up. "One of the waiters will bring some food to you here." He indicated a small room off the passage. Then, meeting her eyes, the mocking glance returned. "Surely you did not suppose those starving women in the ward would allow you to keep anything for yourselves, did you?"

"Hidden beneath my cloak, I hoped——"

"For a bite of decent food they would tear you apart like wolves," he said harshly. "And who could blame them?" His hand on her arm tightened. "Remember what I have told you. Plot, plan, but get out—one way or another!" He swept her a bow, and the sardonic grin was back. "And if we do not meet again, madam, let me say I have never met a more charming—or less accomplished—thief."

Turning abruptly he went back to his guests.

By June, the highwayman Jack Winston was only a memory in the minds of Londoners—a gallant figure who had ridden to his death at Tyburn with a gentleman's courage and grace. In the women's ward of Newgate he was extolled as a hero—the women's brothers, husbands, lovers, all now had known the dashing thief or had shared in his daring exploits. Stories were repeated of the loot he had left behind him—fabulous jewels hidden in a hollow oak—gold and silver buried beneath marked stones in a country churchyard. On moonlit nights his ghost was said to ride a great black mare along the Holbourn Road. Such tales were always told of romantic and tragic figures, Katharine knew, but, like the others, she mourned the thief—less for his reckless ways than for his wasted and profligate life, which order and discipline might have made so different.

To her his legacy had been: *"Plot, plan, but get out!"* The words beat in her memory. Now, alert to any change, aware of each innovation, she watched and waited, timing the comings and goings of the turnkeys, observing the habits of the keepers, searching for a weak link in the chain of routine that encircled her. The doors of the wards were opened by eight every morning, closed by nine at night. Since the piemen and vendors roamed the prison freely during these hours, the great gates of the prison did not close before nine. Escape would be easiest in the evening hours, when the card playing was most riotous, the guests most numerous. And she must not fail. To be caught, to be incarcerated in the small stone cell reserved for recalcitrant prisoners—to be confined alone for unnumbered days —no, she must not fail.

Mary now read aloud each day with a pride in her accomplishment that to her teacher was deeply gratifying. Since she was not content to confine herself to one or two psalms, the older girl sometimes stumbled badly over new words, sounding them out syllable by syllable, until she mastered them. And to her reading Mary had begun to add another achievement. By relinquishing one or two more pennies, Katharine had induced Goss to procure a slate and a handful of chalk. Now she had begun to teach Mary the rudiments of writing also.

This afternoon, while Billy amused himself by winding and rewinding one of his shoes in Katharine's shawl, his mother labored over the letters of her name.

"Perhaps I should have an easier name," she muttered wryly, trying to get the R in *FLETCHER* to her satisfaction.

Katharine laughed in sympathy. "You have come a long way, Mary. Someday you'll be writing letters to your friends!"

"Sooner than ye think, maybe." Mary put the slate aside and brushed the chalk dust from her hands. "Rumors fly thick and fast here, but some say a ship sails this week."

"Oh." Katharine sank down upon the cot. "Oh," she whispered again. "I—I cannot bear to think of life here without you."

"It's not a thing to think about," Mary answered brusquely. "Ye've got to put yer mind to other things —like gettin' away."

"I am," she replied quietly.

"Ye are?" Her companion's eyes were alight with interest. But she asked no more. Both of them realized that it was better for Mary not to be told too much. If Katharine escaped, Mary would certainly be questioned. What she did not know, she could not reveal.

There was a clatter at the doorway now, and the turnkey Goss entered. In the ward a hush fell, as if a hawk cast his sharp eye over a covey of helpless birds.

"Those of ye to be transported will go aboard tomorrow," he announced with no preliminaries, "and ye'll take yer belongin's with ye. I'll call out the names—Adams, Cole, Dunstan, Fletcher, Hardy, Jenkins——"

Now the ward came alive. Women, too disheartened an hour earlier to do more than shuffle the length of the room, scrambled about in a frenzy. Tattered gowns were examined, bewailed, examined again. Mary's eyes grew dark with distress as she looked down at her son.

"He's in rags," she whispered.

"We'll make him a new dress," Katharine reassured her.

"What out of?"

"Out of my petticoat."

When she applied to Goss a few minutes later for her thimble and scissors, he regarded her in amused contempt.

"Ain't got 'em now," he said blandly. "Sold 'em."

"Then the money they brought belongs to me," Katharine replied in resolute tones.

He laughed rudely, fixing his thumbs in his belt and rocking backward on his heels.

"How do ye aim to get it?" he challenged. Then, coming closer, he studied her, his small eyes narrowing. "Why do ye want a scissors and thimble anyways?" he demanded.

"I want to make Billy a new dress."

"I can lend ye some scissors—for a price."

Goss would not give the single penny she could offer more than a sneering glance, Katharine knew. He struck

too hard a bargain. Yet she must come up with something. In sudden inspiration she withdrew two or three
brightly colored ribbons from her sewing kit and held
them out, watching him with anxious eyes.

Disdainfully he examined them, then thrust the
whole lot into his pocket. "I'll make ye a loan of some
scissors for ten minutes," he conceded. "Ain't got a
thimble."

While Billy stood wide-eyed and wondering, swathed
in Katharine's shawl, the girl quickly traced a pattern
from his old gown on the folds of her petticoat, then
slashed out the new dress. Taking up her cloak, she
ripped off two of the shoulder capes, and before the
time came to relinquish the scissors, snipped off a strip
of lining from the cloak itself.

With a bewildered frown, Mary watched. "What are
ye doin' that for?" she asked.

"Be patient," Katharine said, smiling at her. "You'll
see."

Taking a spool of black thread from her kit, she
broke off a length, thrust it through a needle and began to attach one of the capes to the other. From the
strip of lining she fashioned two long strings, sewing
them at either edge of the neck. Then she held up the
result of her labors—a small cape for Billy.

"Oh." Mary's eyes filled with tears. "It's beautiful."

"It will keep him warm, at least," Katharine said
practically. "And the cloak is yours, Mary."

"No." Mary shook her head. "I cannot take it. Ye'll

need it here in this damp and cold. Besides, the ship will be warm—most days anyway," she finished doubtfully.

"If you both have cloaks, you can go up on deck when the captain allows it." Katharine threaded the needle with white thread and commenced to work on the dress. "The sea air will be good for Billy," she added deliberately.

Mary was silent. "What about you?" she asked at last.

"I have the shawl."

"It's not much."

"It's enough. I want you to have the bonnet, too. I have no use for it here."

"No, I'll not take that." Mary's voice was resolute. "Ye might be able to sell it sometime."

Katharine laughed. "Who would want it here, pray?"

"Goss might give ye a penny or two for it, if he thought he could sell it at a profit."

"Very well, I shall keep the bonnet." She replaced the bonnet beneath her cot, and watched as Mary put Billy down to rest, his old gown hanging in limp rags about his spindly legs.

Beyond the high, barred windows the sky had already begun to darken with the threat of a storm, and Katharine bent to her task. The new dress must be finished before the light failed, she thought anxiously, for she could not afford a candle. There was no time for the fine stitches she had been taught to take, and with a deft hand she ran up the side seams. Only when Mary's fingers touched hers did she look up from her work.

"Ye've been generous to us," the older girl said softly. "And I thank ye."

Dropping the dress in her lap, Katharine stared up at her friend. "Write to me, Mary," she begged.

"Ye'd never get a letter here," Mary said with a dark frown. Then her brow cleared a little. "But there's Annie Moore at The Bell. I could write to her maybe, and she might get a message to ye."

Not daring to trust her voice, Katharine nodded, and swiftly lifting the dress again, she resumed her work.

Mary picked up the Psalter, turned the pages a minute or two with gentle hands, and then began, a little hesitantly, to read aloud.

Though her teacher listened, she did not fully hear the psalm Mary had chosen. Only her pupil's voice moving slowly and triumphantly over the words came to her—like a singer, she thought with a pride and joy that quickened her heart—like a singer, shouting a hymn of victory.

5

Katharine had not anticipated such loneliness. From the moment she awoke in the morning, dreading the sight of the empty cot beside her, until sleep claimed her somewhere in the interminable night, she longed for Mary and her child. Trying to dull the persistent ache and determined to rejoice in their change of fortune, she tried to imagine her friends in their new surroundings—Mary in her cloak, Billy in his cape—reveling in the sunshine and sea air. But such a picture, she knew, was distorted. It would be a rare ship's captain indeed who concerned himself with the well-being of his prisoners, other than to keep them alive until the end of the voyage. And the visions of sunlight and sea she conjured up only emphasized her own miserable surroundings.

Most of the women remaining in the ward were inmates of long standing. Katharine would have found it hard to join their small cliques, even had she wanted to. But to the noisy card games and constant wrangling, she preferred solitude. And with increased fervor she tried to concentrate on some means of freeing herself from this wretched place.

Now that many of the women had boarded the transports, a little more money jingled in the ward. These pennies had been extorted from the wretches assigned to sail, whose pride or necessity had forced them to purchase a thrifty neighbor's rags to cover their own nakedness.

This early July evening a pieman made his rounds, his cry of "Toss and buy! Up and win 'em!" enticing many of the women to gamble. The pieman never tossed the coin, but if he called correctly, he then won the penny and kept the pie. If he lost, he handed over the pie for nothing.

Now, holding out his tray of pies, spicy in the humid air, he approached Katharine. Slight of build, he was no bigger than a boy, the girl observed, with his pieman's cap set at a rakish angle on dark, curly hair caught back in a queue. Nothing but his tray of pies and his breeches, shirt, and cap marked him, outwardly at least, from the rest of them. And in a flash she saw her means of escape. In his clothes she herself might move in—or out—of the prison.

"Pie?" He grinned at her.

She nodded, too overcome with the excitement of her scheme to speak. It was madness, of course, to risk her last penny, but she must detain him, talk with him a little. With trembling fingers she dug in her pocket and brought up the money.

"Is—is business good?"

He shook his head. "Not worth me while comin' 'ere in the wards."

"Where do you go usually?"

"Mostly in the press yard, and where the rich ones 'ave their rooms."

"Do you—do you need a password to get in and out?"

"Lord, no." Again he grinned. "They knows me by now. That turnkey, Goss, he remembers everyone. Eyes like an eagle's. I comes in the front and I goes out that way—just before they close up at nine." His eyes narrowed as he recalled his business with her. "Are ye tossin'?"

"Yes." She threw the penny into the air.

"Heads!" he called.

The luck of the toss gave him the penny, and with a shrug he picked up his tray of pies and moved on.

Most of that night and all of the next day she racked her brains for some means of coming by a pieman's cap, a ragged shirt, and breeches. It might be possible to buy them, of course, if she had the money. Money, always money! Frustrated, she flung herself off the cot and ran out into the passageway to pace along its narrow walls. If only she could discuss her plan with someone she could trust! If only she had a few shillings to her name!

Dinner that day was particularly nauseating. Scraps of beef, gray with age, and bread, moldy from the dampness, made up the meal. Katharine fingered the food listlessly. Where had her anger gone? she wondered, and realized with a jolt that outrage required energy, and her own passions were growing as weak and thin as the body that encompassed them. This thought was terrifying, and in a sudden burst of vigor she thrust the food away and moved out into the corridor again.

Goss's gaze was on her here, his small dark eyes calculating as always. A shudder of revulsion seized her. What did he want? she asked herself uneasily as he approached her now, walking on the balls of his feet as softly and noiselessly as a cat.

"Ye got a visitor in the hall downstairs—been there quite a while," he said complacently.

"Why didn't you inform me?" she demanded, outraged at his callousness.

"What's the hurry? Ye ain't goin' anywheres special, are ye now?" His stubby fingers touched her arm, and her flesh crawled. "Besides, it'll cost ye sixpence to go down, and another penny to light the way."

"I haven't got sixpence."

"I know it. That's why I didn't hurry to tell ye."

"Is it a man or a woman?"

"Can't say." He looked at her speculatively. "Leastways, not without the sixpence."

Hatred, black and burning, flamed up in her with an intensity so fierce that for a moment she was blinded by it. Like a cat playing with a mouse—a great tomcat, powerful and vain—Goss now tossed her about at his will. What did he expect? That she would beg? That she would weep? That she would borrow from him, placing herself irrevocably in his debt?

Striving to regain her self-possession, she said nothing. When she did speak at last, she managed to keep her voice casual and unconcerned.

"I have something worth a great deal more than sixpence," she murmured.

"What?"

"A bonnet."

"Who wants a bonnet?"

With a shrug she began to stroll slowly toward the ward. "Who wants to see visitors?" she countered.

He followed her a few steps. "He looks like a gentleman."

Her heart leaped, but she gave no indication of her excitement.

He was beside her now. "Where's the bonnet?"

"By my cot."

"Get it."

Even now she did not allow herself to hurry, and

when she returned with the bonnet, Goss was impatient.

"Took yer time about it," he exclaimed irritably.

Katharine spun the bonnet on her finger, watching the pale ostrich plumes wave languidly.

"Just like the quality wears," he muttered, touching a plume.

"Yes," she agreed.

"I'll give ye sevenpence for it, enough to light ye down and pay yer fee in."

"And how do I get back?"

"If ye need more, get *him* to pay it," he said with a leer, counting the money into her hand.

A moment later she picked her way down the stone stairs by the candle's flame, pausing at the foot to quiet her racing heart. Then she went on, hesitantly now, conscious of her stained and filthy gown, her stale and unwashed body. Would she ever be clean again—really clean, with fresh linen cool and sweet against her flesh?

A turnkey gathered up the sixpence at the door of the stone hall where visitors and prisoners mingled in noisy confusion. Katharine cast a cursory glance among them; then, as no familiar figure met her gaze, she searched again, her eyes regarding each and every person slowly, intently, while panic rose in her heart like a drowning wave. Had he gone?

The touch on her shoulder was so welcome that she spun round, speechless, to stare up at Michael Edes—seeing the same handsome face, pale now and gaunt to the bone, the same dark eyes, tender and smiling. Clasping her hands tightly within his own, the doctor raised them to his lips and drew her close. Within the circle of his arms she stood quiet, so overwhelmed that in relief and happiness she burst into tears.

"My dear Miss Leslie, are you aware that you are ruining my neckcloth?" The gentle hand upon her hair belied the raillery of his words. Katharine drew back a little.

"I—I am so happy to see you, sir," she stammered. "I feared you had forgotten me."

He gave a low laugh. "Quite the contrary, I assure you. I have thought of little else. Unfortunately, a week or two after our meeting, on one of my country calls my horse shied at a rabbit and threw me. My leg was broken—a somewhat complicated fracture that has been slow to heal, not aided, I fear, by an infection that set in." His smile was rueful. "I have been forced to a long holiday I could neither afford nor enjoy. And it was only yesterday that I was able to return to London."

"Oh," she said, comforted.

"Come, let us sit down." He led her to a wall bench and sank down on it with a grateful sigh.

"You must have been very ill," she murmured, noticing his weakness more fully now.

"But I am recovered." His tone was reassuring. "Tell me how I may be of service? Money, of course." Drawing a handful of coins from his pocket, he thrust them into her hands. "And what else?"

"You—you are most generous." Dropping the coins in her pocket, she looked up to send a quick glance round the room. "Do you think you could get me a pieman's cap and clothes?" she whispered, and at his look of bewilderment hurriedly outlined her plan.

When she had finished, his eyes meeting hers were bright and intense. "God grant it works—and it must work," he said grimly. "Even though the prison is being 'improved' and made 'more commodious'"—his lips curled round the incongruous words of the prison renovators—"jail fever is rife on the debtors' side, and it is only a question of time before it reaches you." His eyes flicked over the room, and he bent closer. "When do you mean to break out?"

"As soon as I can."

"First you will need shelter." She was warmed anew by his instant acceptance of her plan and his ready willingness to help. "I live some distance away, at my sister's house in Bloomsbury Square. At present she is not at home, but her housekeeper is an ingenious woman and completely trustworthy, so you will be safe with us." He thought for a minute. "Can you meet me at the west side of St. Paul's—near the statue of Queen Anne?"

"Yes." She nodded. "I know St. Paul's, and the statue is of white marble."

"I shall be there three nights from now—counting

tonight as the first night." His brows drew together in a frown. "But can you find your way if it is nearly dark?"

"I can always hear the bells chime the hours and the quarters."

"Of course." His face cleared.

"But you——" She sent him an anxious glance. "Are you recovered enough to——"

"Do not consider me, I beg," he responded quickly. "You will need every ounce of your strength and guile to get out of this place. Runners will be out as soon as your absence is noticed—for God's sake, take care." He rose, and Katharine stood, too, feeling a new confidence as she looked up at him. "If I am to serve you best, it is wisest that we not be seen together again," he said, and then, as her face betrayed her disappointment, he gave a little laugh and caught up her hands. "Have faith in me, please. Within the next two days I shall somehow contrive to get the clothes to you." He moved toward the door. "Can you find your way safely back to the ward?"

"Oh, yes." She dipped in a curtsy. "And I do thank you," she murmured gratefully, "for the money and all else."

He bowed. "God keep you."

A day later she again made her way down the stairs, Goss this time at her side, one thick hand on her arm, the other holding a candle to light their way.

"Ye've got some strange friends," he muttered.

"This woman looks like a gypsy, with a shawl half-coverin' her face and a skirt as wide as a tent."

Katharine smiled to herself. Unwittingly he had told her all she needed to know. Now she could find her accomplice with no difficulty.

She had not counted on the turnkey's staying so close to her side, however. Right into the reception hall he accompanied her, accosting the gypsy woman with a suspicious grunt.

"Do ye speak the king's English?"

"Aye, master." The voice was deep and foreign-sounding, as an unusually tall woman with a face as brown as an acorn—the little Katharine could see of it —went down in an awkward curtsy to the jailer.

He seemed satisfied and moved off. Katharine and the stranger sat down on a bench against the wall. In her anxiety the girl scarcely looked at her companion. "Do you have the clothes?" she asked in an urgent whisper.

"Beneath my skirt. I have also this new gown for you, already inspected and approved by a turnkey." A brown finger indicated a gown of green homespun, heavy and voluminous, lying in her lap. "When the sheepdog leaves his flock—" The dark eyes followed Goss as he moved out of the murky room. "Now." From beneath her skirt the gypsy whipped out the garments, tumbling them quickly into the folds of the gown. Katharine found herself holding the pieman's costume, completely concealed in the green dress.

"My thanks," she whispered gratefully.

"God keep you."

With a stifled gasp, she recognized the words and tone of Michael Edes. But before she could respond, the gypsy figure had moved out into the passageway and was out of sight.

Cautiously she made her way back up the stone stairs, her shaking hands clutching the dress close. The ingenuity and daring of the young doctor had stunned her; his total disregard for the risk he himself was incurring in aiding and abetting a prisoner of the King left her trembling for his safety.

Sometime in the night, when the ward was a murmur of sleep, Katharine slipped into the breeches and shirt, pinning the large cap at her waist. All but a few shillings she transferred to a breeches' pocket. In the other she hid her Psalter. Over this costume she pulled the green gown, blessing whoever had cut the dress so generously that its high neck, long sleeves, and many folds covered her fully.

No new acquisition ever went unremarked in the ward. In the morning the tall, bony woman, acknowledged leader of the group, accosted Katharine.

"There's some of us could use yer old gown," she announced without preamble.

Katharine had anticipated this demand, and although Michael Edes's generous gift had made the selling of her old gown unnecessary, it would be dangerous, she knew, to admit to her new wealth.

"What will you give me for it?" she asked.

Lifting the dress from the cot, the woman examined it. "It's almost in rags," she said disdainfully, "hardly worth a shilling."

"I paid ten shillings to keep it," Katharine retorted, reminded of her humiliating arrival, and angered at the cool assumption she could be so easily cheated.

They eyed each other, and this time Katharine's glance did not waver. She was tempted to retaliate. Yet she could not bring herself to demand an exorbitant fee for the dress, knowing full well that the purchase price would be extorted from the next newcomer who crossed the threshold of the ward.

"Two shillings," she said inexorably.

Surprisingly, the bony hand held out the coins, and Katharine relinquished the dress.

When Goss appeared a short while later, she was expecting him.

"Ye owe me a shilling," he informed her curtly. "Ye well know that half the money changin' hands comes to me."

Katharine longed to throw the money in his face. But she could not risk such a gesture of disdain. Without a word she dropped the coin in his palm.

By early evening she felt as if she had lived a hundred years. Nervously her fingers checked the shillings which she had now placed in the pocket of her new gown, or touched her waist where the cap lay hidden. But she was careful to do nothing that would excite suspicion, and followed the tedious routine as always.

The night was rainy, and the wind brought the bells of St. Paul's close. Eight strokes now from the clock told her that within the next hour she must be out of the prison. Trying to appear as usual, she made her way into the passage where several prisoners strolled about. Katharine passed among them casually, seeking the stairs. At the top of the flight, as she had hoped, she met the curly-haired pieman with his tray of pies.

"Toss or buy! Up and win 'em!" He flung out the words automatically.

She put out a hand and spoke softly. "Will you sell me the whole tray?"

"*What?*"

Thrusting out two shillings, she let them speak for her.

"By heaven and all the saints," he whispered. "Are ye in yer right mind? What do ye want with six pies at four times the price?"

"I want the tray, too," she insisted.

"I'll take 'em to wherever you say and keep the tray," he offered.

"No. I want to surprise someone. It's a wager," she said, lowering her voice to a whisper, and hoping this suggestion would allay his suspicions. "I've got to have the tray, too. You can buy another."

"Aye," he agreed, eyeing the money. "For that sum I can buy three or four!" He plucked up the shillings and quickly moved off.

Balancing the tray in one hand, and clutching at the

wall with the other, Katharine descended the stairs. At the foot she whisked into the dark well beneath the staircase and stripped off the green gown, kicking it into a far corner. Swiftly she tucked her hair beneath the wide band of the cap, then picking up the tray, she moved out into the passage, long and shadowy, with only the oil lamps on the walls sending up their flares of smoky, yellow light.

Afraid that her voice would betray her, she did not dare call out her wares. At the taproom, the air loud with noise and gray with tobacco smoke, she paused, and sidling in, slid three of the pies onto a stone bench. No one paid the least notice. She slipped out again. It was safer to leave a few pies on the tray. Often, she knew, the piemen returned to the street without having sold all of their wares. Now she had only to pass the turnkeys' rooms, be identified as a pieman by the guard on duty, and wait for the great door to swing wide. As she approached the entrance, the passage narrowed, and she felt her heart contract, too, beating in heavy, thick strokes.

"Pieman!"

Out of the stony silence, a voice shook her to a standstill. She turned and saw at the doorway of his room the heavy figure of Goss.

"S-sir?" Even in her own ears her voice sounded tense and high-pitched.

"Two pies."

Katharine approached with the tray, her fingers white

along its edge. Deliberately Goss selected the two largest pies, and she waited for him to toss a penny. But no coin was forthcoming. This, then, was another privilege of the jailer—free food.

She tried to keep her face averted as his eyes moved lazily over her.

"I thought ye'd sold all yer pies to one of the women," he said slowly, and in sickening shock she realized that the pieman had already passed out of the prison for the night.

"I—I came back with more," she stammered.

"Did ye now?" His voice was low, almost a chuckle, and she was not prepared for the thick hand that fell swift and hard as a bludgeon, striking the tray from her hand and scattering its contents along the passage. Then, thrusting upward, it cut the cap from her head to tumble her dark curls about her face and neck.

"Ye almost got away with it, didn't ye?" he taunted, seizing her roughly and yanking her into the small room.

Terror drowned her in a burning tide, and for a moment she went limp with fear beneath his hands. Hard on hers, the jailer's small eyes, triumphant and calculating, seemed to measure her strength, and as he moved closer he relaxed his grip a little. In that instant Katharine wrenched free, twisting round a table and stumbling over a stool as she sprang toward the door. With a grunt of rage Goss lunged after her. With all her might she kicked the stool full in his path. She heard him curse, saw him fling out his arms in an effort to save himself, then sprawl in a bulky heap to lie motionless upon the stone floor, a line of blood trickling from his mouth.

Pulling the door to behind her, she crept out into the passage, caught up the cap and thrust her curls within it, stooped again to pick up the tray. Forcing her trembling knees to obey her, she moved toward the entrance, where, by the dim light of the wall torches she could see another turnkey standing in the shadows.

"Goin' out for the night?"

"Aye," she whispered hoarsely.

"Goss is in charge. He'll open up for ye."

She fought for a breath that would not betray her. "He's got company. I—I just looked."

He gave a low laugh and winked. "Thought I heard voices there a minute ago. Well, we won't disturb 'em."

Cold with terror the girl waited, seeing in her mind's eye Goss, staggering suddenly to his feet, reeling bloody and disheveled into the passage to shout her back. Numbly she stood while the guard with slow, heavy arms let down the bars, shot back the bolt, and fitted the key into the lock. The great door swung wide at last, and she brushed by him into the night.

6

Forcing herself to steadiness, Katharine moved out of the prison yard, her feet neither hasty nor slow, the cap pulled over her brow, the tray tucked under her arm. The rain had ceased, but the cobbles glistened with puddles that soaked quickly through her shoes. Moist and rancid, the air was heavy with the many odors peculiar to these narrow lanes in the heart of London; but after the stale, dead atmosphere of the prison every breath was a joy. Looking up to the dome of St. Paul's, she could see the ball and the cross, a glimmer of gold in the evening sky. And now the great clock of the cathedral struck the half hour, its tones shimmering across the rooftops. But she did not need the clock to guide her. In the twilight it was easy to find the way.

Once beyond the prison she increased her pace. Here in Warwick Lane anyone could safely hurry without remark. People were everywhere this warm July night, and she was one of them. Out of the corner of her eye she saw a crippled bootblack dip into his mixture of egg white and lampblack and apply it vigorously to a gentleman's boots. Across the lane an old woman took a stick to a mongrel foraging in her doorway, sending him sliding and yelping across the cobbles to sniff at Katharine's heels—persistent as a constable, the girl thought in rising panic. How much time had she? Minutes? Hours? When Goss regained consciousness, he would sound the alarm—unless—unless he was dead. Pray God she had not killed him, scoundrel though he was.

She began to run, clutching the tray hard against her side, her fleeing figure casting weird shadows on the mullioned shopwindows of toymakers and booksellers as she fled by. Her breath hot in her throat, she came at last within the west gate of the cathedral, and saw ahead the statue of Queen Anne, ghostly in the fading light. Skirting the pale form, Katharine flung herself with a sob of thankfulness into the arms of Michael Edes.

"Thank God," he murmured, plucking the pieman's cap from her head and enveloping her in a cloak. "Come. I have a cab waiting." His hand on her arm urged her out of the gate and into the waiting cab. Quickly they rolled away.

Her own part in the scheme brought to fruition, now,

in the safety of the cab, she began to tremble uncontrollably.

"What is it?" he asked gently, taking her hands.

Halting at first, her words gradually became coherent, as in horror and revulsion she told him of her escape.

"You are safe now," he murmured reassuringly. Then she felt his hand clutch hers in sudden passion. "But when I consider—" With a harsh laugh he broke off. "Do not dwell on it, I beg. I'll wager the beast is fully alive and even now sending out runners in search of you."

When the cab arrived in Bloomsbury Square, darkness had fallen. Passively she moved up the steps of a brick house, passed through a dark hall and into a panelled room lighted by a sconce of candles. At the window, facing the street, a small, brisk woman snapped the curtains to and came forward, smiling.

"I have been watching for you, Doctor. Everything is in readiness. Hot water, soap, towels—"

Michael Edes's laughter broke across her words, and he smiled down at Katharine.

"We seem always to meet over hot water, do we not? But this will be no less welcome than that which you ordered at the inn, I am sure, and there will be no charge for it." He lifted the cloak from her shoulders. "You will excuse me now, if you please. Mrs. Black will take care of you. When you are refreshed, we can talk."

An hour later, fresh petticoats swirling beneath a gown of cornflower blue, her feet incased in velvet slippers, she joined Michael Edes in the small parlor. In the glow from the candles her skin shone like pale satin, and her hair gleamed blue-black. A ruffle of lace at the neck of her bodice and at the edge of either sleeve lent an accent of elegance to the simple muslin gown. In the mirror behind him she saw herself suddenly transformed, and her eyes, dark blue, enormous with excitement and pleasure, sought her host's, finding his glance warmly admiring.

"The ugly duckling," he murmured, "now the swan." Taking her arm, he led her to a sofa. "Pray be seated, ma'am." He drew a small table close. "Mrs. Black has prepared a little supper for us. Are you hungry?"

Katharine shook her head. Meeting him on equal ground, she found herself overwhelmed by his courtesy and thoughtfulness and could not answer.

"I prescribe a nourishing meal, nonetheless." He seated himself opposite her, his dark eyes intent on her face. "Is something wrong?" he asked quietly.

"You—you have been so generous to me," she said helplessly. "The money, the pieman's clothes, the very garments I am now wearing——"

"You do me too much honor. Surely you do not regard me as a connoisseur of lady's finery?" His eyes teased her. "Mrs. Black made up the green gown from my description of you," he continued more seriously as he ladled soup from a tureen into a bowl and gave it to her. "The clothes you have on are my sister's. I regret that she cannot be here to welcome you this evening, but while her husband is abroad, she is visiting with friends in the country." He appraised her again with a warm glance that held a hint of laughter. "Allow me to say that in size and fit the blue gown is well-nigh perfect!"

With a blush she turned the subject quickly to him. "How did you come by the gypsy disguise?"

"Ah." A grin touched his mouth. "A little dye on my skin, a huge skirt—again Mrs. Black's deft needle—one or two scarves and shawls judiciously draped, and I had all that was needed. It will be difficult to find the gypsy woman, when the search for accomplices begins." He laughed softly, and she suspected that the bafflement of the prison authorities would add an extra fillip to the risk he had run.

"You think they will search at once?" A quiver of dread ran through her.

"Yes. Finding you will be a matter of pride with Goss. That is one reason why I am sending you out of the country tomorrow. I want you to be safe."

Katharine put down her spoon, apprehension swallowing her meager appetite.

"Out—out of the country?" she faltered.

"Because there is no lasting safety for you here. Come, eat up your supper," he said firmly. "Then we can talk at length."

Obediently she swallowed the soup. He rang the bell, and after Mrs. Black had cleared away the things, came to sit beside her on the sofa.

"Tomorrow morning the wife of Captain Thompson —he is a good friend and master of one of my cousin's ships, the *Claire*—will call for you here in her carriage. You will appear to be my sister going out for a ride in the park. Actually Mrs. Thompson will take you aboard the *Claire*, which sails on the noon tide, assuming that the wind is in the right quarter, of course."

Katharine listened intently as he continued.

"My sister, meanwhile, is expected back here around noon. Thus, anyone seeing you leave and noting her arrival later may well believe it to be the same person, since you will be dressed much alike and are so near a height and size. I think we may assume no one saw you arrive this evening, and the cabby won't betray us; he is an old friend of mine. I am taking these precautions because the house may soon be watched, if the authorities suspect me as an accomplice. In prison you had only two visitors, did you not? The gypsy woman and myself?"

She nodded, appalled at the added risk he must sustain because of her. "How—how much danger is there for you?" she whispered.

"Almost none, I think. But there are always informers. And I am known in the prison. I have visited there many times. In some ways prison can be an excellent training ground for a doctor."

Katharine nodded.

"If my plans do not miscarry, by midmorning tomorrow you will be safe aboard the *Claire*," he continued.

"Captain Thompson carries letters to my cousin, a widower who lives with his mother and daughter in Falmouth. You will recall that the Falmouth I refer to is a part of the Colony of Massachusetts—a small town lying on the coast of Maine some hundred or more miles to the northeastward of Boston." He paused a moment and smiled. "Do not imagine that it compares with London. But my cousin has a comfortable home there, and will, I am sure, find a place for you in his household. There you will be out of harm's way."

Again he paused, and she waited for him to go on. "Annette has been in need of a good teacher for some time. That is why I think my cousin will welcome you so readily. In my letter I have told him that you have taught in a nobleman's family." His glance met hers and held an instant. "I have *not* told him the reason you left Lady Blaize's employ. I ask you to do that."

"But—but is it necessary?"

"Yes. We must be honest. Once Edmund has seen you, however, and the work I believe you can accomplish with his daughter Annette—" He broke off, but his smile was reassuring. "I do not imagine that your references, or lack of them, will make any great difference."

"Then I shall not see you again," she said with regret.

"I must complete my studies here and attend to my practice, at least a little longer. I hope to return to Falmouth in late winter or early spring."

He spoke with a confidence that inspired her trust,

and now her curiosity leaped to the household in America. Turning to him, she voiced the first question that sprang to her mind.

"Are you alike, sir—your cousin and you?"

He threw back his head and laughed. "I had forgot I am dealing with a female mind!" Though his eyes regarded her in amused tolerance, he answered her question in all seriousness. "No, ma'am, we are not alike. In principle my cousin and I are the same, perhaps. But in politics we differ. Edmund is a King's man to the core. I am not. But my cousin is a man of courage and of honor, you will find—handsome, too, though a little heavy perhaps." His dark eyes mocked her now. "I must in all honesty confess that he is not young—thirty-six, I believe."

Katharine laughed a little, too, but within, her heart misgave her. Would this stranger, older and obviously well-established, welcome her into his household as readily as her host imagined? Might he not consider her too young and inexperienced a teacher for his only child? How would he react to the story of her imprisonment? Still, Michael Edes's great kindness to her demanded a faith in his judgment. Besides, she had no choice. England held no refuge for her.

Rising, she shook out the folds of her borrowed gown and again looked out over the small room, so cozy and secure against the perils of the night. Was this the reality, she wondered, scarcely daring to believe it, and prison now the dream?

Her host had risen, too, and lighting a candle in the flames of the wall sconce, he led her up the stairs. The cuffs of his coat were worn thin and threadbare, she saw beneath the gleam of yellow light, and earlier she had noticed how carefully darned were his black stockings. Much of what he had given her might so easily have been spent on his own wardrobe, she reflected in a rush of gratitude.

Beyond the landing he stopped at the open door of a chamber.

"Mrs. Black is just across the hall, should you need her," he said in low tones, handing Katharine the candle.

"Thank you." Stirred anew by her happy escape and his part in it, she put her hand in his and spoke from her heart. "I owe you more than I can ever express," she said earnestly.

His face was in shadow as he looked down at her, but she saw his smile. "I shall demand no payment," he replied, touching his lips to her fingers, "except that you not forget me, Katharine."

PART TWO

7

On a brilliant morning in late August, 1774, the *Claire* sailed into Casco Bay, and by afternoon the sturdy ship was moored at one of the Falmouth wharves. To the captain and crew Falmouth was home, and the excitement of return spread like a flame through the ship, encompassing even Katharine, who stood alone at the rail, staring out into the town with its cluster of wooden houses, its two lonely church spires, and its forest of trees—a ring of variegated greens to the north and the west. How small it was, like a toy village—and how different from London!

"It's a good place to come back to." Beside her, Tom Lawrence, third mate and nephew to the Captain, spoke proudly. Grateful to be included in the fever of homecoming, Katharine turned to him, feeling suddenly very unsure of herself and beset with doubts. Following his glance, she watched the Captain's wife dip in a curtsy as a tall, imposing man came aboard.

"Edmund Winter," Tom explained. "He's the owner of the *Claire*. You are going to make your home with him and his mother in King Street, I understand?"

"I hope so."

"He is a fine man, though he is a Tory. But I don't envy you trying to teach that chit Annette! She's made of greased lightning!"

It was the Captain himself who presented Katharine to Edmund Winter some time later.

"I am honored." As he bowed over her hand, Mr. Winter sent a swift glance over her slight figure in its gray linen gown, black shawl, and pale pink bonnet. His clubbed wig was neat above his bright, blue eyes; his face, though fleshy and dark-veined, was kindly in its expression. "I have just read my cousin's letter concerning you." His smile erased some of her fears. "I must confess I have never had a governess bestowed upon me under quite these circumstances, but I have a good bit of faith in my cousin's judgment, and I am willing to give you a trial."

Katharine curtsied. "Thank you, sir," she murmured gratefully.

He turned to the Captain and his wife. "You will give me the pleasure of your company at dinner tomorrow? I am counting on it."

"You will see us both, Edmund." Captain Thompson grinned. "I remember Polly's cooking—none better!" He bowed to Katharine. "Good day, Miss Leslie. Happy to have had you aboard. I will see that your bag reaches you within the hour."

"Thank you, sir." She dipped again and then turned to his wife. "And I thank you, madam, for your generous care of me during the voyage."

Gathering up her skirts, she crossed the narrow gangplank and set her feet on land, her first steps quick and decisive. Then, without warning, the wharf rose alarmingly, and her hold on Edmund Winter's arm tightened in panic.

With a laugh he steadied her. "Your sea legs are still with you, I see. Stand still a moment and get your bearings."

Motionless, she stared stolidly out into the town, feeling the dizziness gradually subside.

"Now take a deep breath," he commanded.

Katharine obeyed, sniffing up the fragrant scent of spices from a nearby warehouse, smelling, too, the odor of fish and tar and rope as they began to walk along the wharf.

"Better?"

"Yes, thank you, sir." She looked up to find his expression very grave, almost frowning.

"You are very young, Miss Leslie," he said slowly, "and although my cousin assures me that your training has been excellent, I am not at all sure that you will do."

Katharine's fears flooded back, and she listened appre-
hensively. "My daughter has had a succession of governesses—not easy to come by in a small provincial
town, believe me. Except for my mother—who should
not be expected to undertake this task—Annette has
been without a teacher some five months now. Were I
not desperate, I should consider you far too young and
inexperienced an instructor for a child of twelve. As it
is, I am willing that you try. But I must warn you that
you will find your pupil sadly in need of discipline." His
voice sounded a little less stern now, almost apologetic.
"She is an only child, and since her mother's death five
years ago, I fear I have been far too indulgent with her."

"That is natural, sir, I suppose," Katharine murmured
politely.

"Perhaps. At any rate, though I most decidedly did
not expect you, let me say that you are most welcome.
We can arrange about your wages at a more convenient
time, if it please you."

"Yes, thank you, sir." She felt as if she had been
thrust back a little way from the edge of a precipice.
"Believe me, I am deeply grateful to you for receiving
me, unexpected and unknown to you, with such grace."

They had arrived at the end of the wharf, and now
turned into a busy street filled with carts and wagons.
Mr. Winter guided her close to the buildings, but despite his care a young man, garbed in dirty buckskins,
suddenly veered from his path and brushed her arm
rudely. Astonished, she drew up.

"I beg your pardon, ma'am." The gray eyes meeting hers were insolent, the bow mocking. Withdrawing as abruptly as he had appeared, the youth continued down the street.

"*Cad!*" Edmund Winter's voice was thick with fury, his face livid with anger.

"Surely it was an accident," Katharine exclaimed, astounded at his passion.

"I wish I might think so!" He drew a deep breath, and taking her hand placed it securely within his arm. "No, he is one of the rebels, 'Liberty Boys,' they call themselves, bent on humbling his betters—those of us who are King's men. It was a deliberate insult, Miss Leslie, more to me than to you."

She looked at him in bewilderment. "But why?"

"He knows I will not risk a street brawl. Nor can I easily call out a man half my age. Men do not duel here quite so readily, perhaps, as in England. He is well aware, too, that for me to seek redress through the law is to receive more abuse from his friends."

"But the royal magistrates——"

"Here there is no King's justice, ma'am. The law is now in the hands of a Committee of Safety, a Committee of Inspection." His voice grew caustic. "These men, such as the cad who just insulted you, are half of them debtors, the other half jailbirds who shout for liberty. I am sick to death of lawbreakers," he finished in bitter tones.

Katharine was shaken. All during the voyage she had

looked forward to the moment when her feet would walk firmly on the solid brown earth of this new land, finding it a haven and a refuge for her own misfortunes. Boston, she knew, was full of rebels. Parliament had shut up the port to punish them; General Gage was in command. But she had never expected to find this small town to the eastward rebellious, divided between Loyalist and rebel. Was there no security anywhere?

From under her lashes she stole a glance at her new employer, seeing his mouth pulled firm in a hard, uncompromising line. She had intended to follow Michael's advice and confess at once to her own turbulent background. But if Edmund Winter thought her too young, if she was only on trial, if his feelings were so strongly aroused—surely it would be more prudent, at least for the time being, to hold her peace.

Now they crossed into another street, and here the houses, though all of wood, were impressive. Painted red, most of them were set a little back from the road. Coach houses stood at the rear, and beyond these, orchards reached to the dark woods that rose tall and close. Before a three-storied house, red like its neighbors, its paned windows reflecting sun and shadow, Edmund Winter unlatched a gate and held it wide. Katharine passed through onto a path of beach pebbles, hard and clean. No longer need she clutch up her skirts, and letting them fall, she put out a hand to touch a blossom of Queen Anne's lace close beside the path. The familiar flower was like the welcome of an old friend.

The door was flung open by a Negro servant, who took his master's hat and gloves.

"When Miss Leslie's bag arrives, see that it is put in the back chamber, Rome."

"Yes, sir."

"Father!" The voice that accosted them was high-pitched in surprise, and looking up Katharine saw a young girl halfway down the stairs. Blond hair hung in a thick fall to the waist of her pale summer frock, and the blue eyes staring into Katharine's were wide in surprise.

"Come down and meet your new governess, Annette." Her father spoke with a smile.

Reluctantly the girl descended the stairs, trailing a hand along the banister. "I did not know I was to have a new governess," she pouted.

"Nor did I. But you cannot live in ignorance forever. She is a present from Michael."

"Michael!" In a flash the small face changed from petulance to pleasure. Her whole being quickened, and she flew down the remaining stairs in a flurry of petticoats. "Did he send a message?" she demanded of Katharine.

"Mind your manners, miss, if you please!" her father said sharply. "Miss Leslie, may I present my daughter, Annette."

Annette went down in a swift curtsy, like the dip of a butterfly, and held out her hand. But the curt reproof made little impression. "Did he send a message, ma'am?" she repeated.

Katharine could recall no specific message, but neither could she blight such longing. "He asked that I give you his warmest regards," she said with a smile, keeping the small, tense hand in hers an extra moment.

"Not his love?"

"Annette!" Edmund Winter exclaimed. "Enough of this nonsense! Take Miss Leslie to her room at once, if you please." He turned to Katharine. "When you are refreshed, I should like to see you in the schoolroom, ma'am."

The chamber on the second floor was at the back of the house, its windows facing north and east.

"There is always a breeze in the summertime," Annette said, indicating the windows. "But it can be cold in winter. However, Rome or one of the stable boys will see that you have wood for the fireplace." She closed the door. "Oh, look! Your bag has arrived. May I watch you unpack?"

"Of course." The older girl smiled as she untied the strings of her bonnet and laid it with her shawl and gloves on the bed. "But I fear you may be disappointed," she warned gently, looking into Annette's eager face. She brought out the blue muslin gown and velvet slippers, also a workgown of figured calico, and a scarlet cloak and hood bestowed upon her by the doctor. Next came a black wool frock she herself had made during the voyage from a bolt of material the Captain's

wife had generously shared. Two extra pairs of stockings and one or two undergarments, all gifts from Mrs.
Black, came last. The gray linen gown she stood up in,
her shoes and stockings, had once belonged to Michael
Edes's sister, as well as the bonnet, shawl, and gloves.

"Is that *all?*"

Katharine laughed. "I said that you would be disappointed, did I not?" As she looked into the dismayed
face of her new charge, she could not resist teasing her
a little. "Now you must be very frank with me. Dare I
appear in the evening in any of these—or are they all
too modest?"

Annette did not return her smile but studied the
dresses in all seriousness. "The blue muslin will do," she
said at last. "I can always lend you my yellow shawl.
Then you will be more presentable."

The interview with Edmund Winter a few minutes
later was cordial. He wished his daughter to study history, composition, music, drawing, and to acquire some
proficiency in arithmetic. Together he and Katharine
selected from the small library of books on the schoolroom shelves the volumes that would be most useful.
*Grammar Made Familiar to Young Gentlemen, Ladies
and Foreigners*, together with *Arithmetic Made Familiar and Easy to Young Gentlemen and Ladies*, both volumes from John Newbery's *The Circle of the Sciences*,
were well known to her. *The Universal Spelling Book* by
Daniel Fenning had been indispensable to Miss Perkins, the governess who had preceded her, said Mr.

Winter. But despite its use, Annette's spelling had not markedly improved.

Nor could he discover that his daughter had as yet read any of William Shakespeare's plays. Surely she could be tempted with *As You Like It* or *A Midsummer Night's Dream?* Her drawing was imaginative, he admitted, showing her new teacher one or two sweeping water colors. Her performance on the harpsichord was not even tolerable, however, because she would not practice.

Then, suggesting that Katharine rest until dinnertime, he dismissed her.

Upstairs the girl examined her new chamber in leisure, finding it spacious indeed after the cramped quarters of the ship. Someone had considerately lighted a fire, and its warmth was welcome, for the day, though bright, was cool. Now she noticed the braided rug beneath her feet and the comfortable wing chair beside the hearth. A large pine chest held extra blankets. There was a walnut clothespress for her gowns and a warming pan for her bed, and the candleholder on the night table boasted two fat, new candles. Drawing back the patchwork quilt, she plunged her hand deep into the feather mattress, feeling it plump up round her fingers. How different from the prison cot! Pray God that Mary and Billy at the end of their voyage had met with fortune as pleasant as this.

Would she find safety and security at last in this strange little colonial town? Certainly everything seemed serene, except for that disturbing incident in the street. Recalling her new employer's stinging condemnation of rebels and convicts, she shuddered. Not every man or woman convicted in the King's court was guilty, as she well knew. Surely Edmund Winter acknowledged exceptions?

Standing on the hearth, she drew off her shoes and gown and stood in her petticoat, staring into the fire. For one awful moment the prison walls rose in the flames, and turning quickly back to the room, Katharine forced herself once more to take stock. Beneath her fingers the linen pillowcase was cool and clean, and the mahogany bedpost was solid in her grip. She turned back to the fire and felt its comfort creep round her in seductive waves of warmth. Gradually her misgivings diminished. Suddenly she was overwhelmed with drowsiness, and pulling up the quilt she stretched out with a sigh of content as deep and soft as her bed.

Although by nine o'clock each morning Katharine sat ready and waiting in the small room off the drawing room designated as the schoolroom, Annette was almost never on time to her lessons. There were innumerable excuses. The new kitten was crying for her milk; it would be cruel to let her go hungry. The parakeet's cage must be cleaned; her grandmother had complained of it. This morning a wasp had flown into her chamber. Ten precious minutes had been devoted to tracking him down and slaying him, Annette herself always in imminent danger of being stung, as she explained breathlessly now to her teacher.

"Your lessons begin at nine," Katharine said inexorably. "If you are late again, we shall work an extra half hour in the afternoon."

Annette pouted. "Miss Perkins never did that," she countered.

Miss Perkins had been putty in her pupil's hands, Katharine reflected inwardly.

But if her pupil was unpunctual, she was in no other respect slow. Annette's quick mind totaled a column of figures with amazing swiftness and astonishing inaccuracy.

"Add it again, if you please." Katharine requested.

"But I've done it four times already!"

"You have yet to arrive at the correct answer."

"Miss Perkins sometimes told me the answers," Annette murmured, casting a sidelong glance at her teacher.

Katharine's lips twitched, but she did not respond otherwise, remaining resolute and unmoving under Annette's scrutiny.

"Oh, very well!" The younger girl's tone was one of injured resignation. Carefully she added up the column again, checked it, and presented the correct answer.

Annette's attention would have been easier to retain had the house provided a more quiet refuge. But almost every day loud voices could be heard in the drawing room, berating the newly elected town officers and com-

plaining bitterly of discrimination. This autumn afternoon the voices had been uglier than usual, Katharine
thought, as she closed the history book and looked at
her pupil.

"Shall we take our exercise now?" she asked.

"Oh, yes!" Springing up happily, Annette tumbled
her books about her.

Garbed in their cloaks, for the September day was
cool, they set off up King Street. When they reached the
top they turned into Back Street; once, more elegantly
termed Queen, Annette confided as she led Katharine
along. The older girl was astonished at the number of
people whom she saw in this neighborhood.

"What is going on?" she exclaimed.

For men in large numbers, some of them armed with
muskets, were hurrying down the short lane that led off
Back Street to the Town House.

"They've come to town to humble Sheriff Tyng." Annette's eyes flashed angrily. "I heard Father and his
friends talking about it this morning."

Katharine hesitated, but Annette would not be de-
terred, and in a moment they were on the edge of a
large crowd, all of whom seemed to be attentively listening to a man standing on the step of the Town House.

"It's Sheriff Tyng," Annette whispered.

The sheriff wore a gold-laced hat which Katharine assumed to be his badge of office, and he stood straight
and tall as he read from a paper in his hand. They could

not hear what he said, but from the roar of approval that went up, they knew when he had finished.

Suddenly both girls were caught up in a throng of men muttering in threatening tones as they pressed toward a nearby tavern. Katharine drew Annette hastily to the opposite side of the lane.

"I should never have brought you here!" she exclaimed, vexed at her own carelessness. "What a disagreeable mob!"

"We are perfectly safe." Annette's self-possession rarely deserted her.

The man in the gold-laced hat was walking slowly in their direction, surrounded by gesticulating friends. Among them Katharine recognized Edmund Winter, and he at that instant saw them.

He came up swiftly. "Annette! Miss Leslie! What brings you here?" he demanded.

"I persuaded Katharine to come in this direction," Annette explained.

"I am very sorry, sir," Katharine apologized. "I had not realized the danger."

"Perhaps it's as well that you see us as we are," her employer said with a heavy sigh. "Sheriff Tyng has just been forced to declare himself no longer a servant of Parliament and the King, but to act only on the consent of the county. That is, he must ignore the recent acts of Parliament—which, by the way, he is sworn to uphold—and instead bow to the will of these unruly men."

"But what is it these men are protesting against?" Katharine asked in bewilderment.

"Parliament has revoked the Massachusetts Charter insofar as electing councilors is concerned. The royal governor now has the power to appoint and remove judges, sheriffs, and other officers without the consent of the Council. Jurors, too, will no longer be elected, but will be summoned by sheriffs. And town meetings cannot be held without the leave of the governor in writing." He guided them round a rough cart track before he concluded. "This is an attempt on the part of Parliament to bring this rebellious element under control."

As they turned into King Street, Katharine studied again the impressive dwellings with their neat pebble walks, handsome doorways, and sparkling windows. Here dwelt the quality—merchants, lawyers, ships' captains. The men she had just seen in leather breeches and linsey-woolsey shirts crowding into Mrs. Greele's tavern had no place here, certainly. How dare such riffraff oppose the King's laws? In Newgate there had been ugly mutterings, bitterly disparaging of the royal magistrates, often abusive of the King himself. But although, like the others, her own initial outrage had been directed at the judge who had condemned her, Katharine's personal wrath had never been leveled at the King. Loyalty to the Crown was a dictum too deeply imposed. And if in the dark recesses of her despair she had occasionally questioned such blind allegiance, now in the light of her freedom she saw the King's laws responsible for a discipline and order she knew and respected. In her eyes the men of Falmouth who protested and rebelled against the dictates of the Crown came close to treason.

At their own gate Edmund Winter paused, swept off his hat, and bowed. "If you will excuse me, I must attend to business at the warehouse," he said.

The two girls bobbed in curtsies, and then proceeded up the path and into the house.

8

As the weeks wore into months, Katharine's fears that she would prove an inadequate teacher in Edmund Winter's eyes gradually diminished. There was no further talk of her being on trial, and her youth, at first considered a handicap, came to be regarded as an asset, since it made her an acceptable companion as well as teacher to Annette. If her pupil's constant company was sometimes exhausting, she did not complain. And she welcomed the lessening of formality which by degrees gave way to a friendly intimacy between governess and family. The schoolroom was a bleak place in which to dine alone, as Annette early pointed out to her father, who henceforth included Katharine at family meals. And since his daughter had almost immediately adopted her governess's given name as her means of address, both Edmund Winter and his mother soon found themselves slipping into the same easy habit.

It was Mrs. Winter who supported Katharine most heartily in her strict regime. As bright as her granddaughter, and quite as resourceful, her dark eyes keen beneath a widow's cap of black lace, the elderly matron upheld the young teacher's insistence on regular hours and steady work habits.

"My son has always been far too occupied with his affairs to look after Annette properly," she confided to Katharine one day soon after the girl's arrival. "He still mourns his wife, you know. Not unnatural, perhaps, but after five years quite impractical."

"Yes, ma'am," Katharine agreed.

"The house needs a younger mistress, if only for Annette's sake," the older woman continued. "I am too old now to assume the discipline and management of a child. And there is a good deal to do besides keeping Annette occupied." Her voice took on a somewhat sharper tone. "The meals must be planned. Edmund prides himself on setting as fine a table as any gentleman of the town!"

To be mistress of such an establishment would be a pleasant task, Katharine mused this November day, as she watched her host carve the brace of chickens set before him. The damask tablecloth was silken to her touch; the heavy silver gleamed. Patterned in pale roses, the new English china was festive. She had yet to grow accustomed to the abundance of foods offered at dinner. Table and sideboard were burdened with buttered potatoes and carrots, creamed parsnips and onions, baked squash, hot breads, jellies, pickles. For dessert there would probably be baked apples, raisins hidden in their sugary depths, cream topping their rosy skins. One russet pear such as adorned the centerpiece would have caused a riot in Newgate, she reflected, feeling a pang for the wretches still imprisoned there. And this plenty was not all. In the evening there would be cold meats, smoked fish, eggs, and tea—despite the rebels' resistance.

She looked up to find her host smiling at her.

"You prefer the white meat, as I recall," he said.

"If you please, sir."

Edmund Winter was as generous as he was kind, she thought gratefully, eyeing the large portion of chicken heaped on her plate. He had offered her a considerably larger wage than she had earned under Lady Blaize. Just yesterday, too, he had made her a gift of rose wool for a new gown, declaring that the bolt could not be put up for sale, since sea water had stained it. But there were many yards without a hint of damage.

After dinner, at the invitation of the family, Katharine retired with them to the drawing room. Settling herself in a deep chair by the fire, Mrs. Winter drew up her feet on a footstool the girl placed for her, arranged her voluminous skirts, and took up her knitting. Preferring a velvet hassock, Katharine drew it to the fire, for rain now beat against the panes with the cold, icy insistence of late autumn, raising a chill dampness along the floor.

Restlessly Annette rubbed at a window. "If only this were snow!" she mourned. "Then Katharine and I could build a snow man or go sledding!"

"Sit down, child, and try not to fret over the good Lord's weather," her grandmother chided. "It has been unusually mild, but it will snow soon enough."

"I have news that will cheer you all!" Edmund Winter held up a hand. "A letter from Michael."

Annette spun away from the window. "Read it, Father! Oh, do, please, read it!" she begged, as she swooped down to gather up the leggy black kitten curling round Katharine's skirts and carry it to the sofa with her.

Her father put on his spectacles, perused the letter a long moment, and then gave a rueful laugh. "Michael's writing has always been atrocious, but he will be with us before too long—that much I can make out readily enough. The rest sounds like the mad ideas of a thorough Whig—largely to do with the Boston Port Bill and its injustice to the inhabitants." His voice hardened a moment. "What a lot our young cousin has to learn!"

He removed his spectacles and looked up at them. "This message came in on one of Captain Pagan's ships yesterday—six weeks out of London. If Michael sails, as he plans, aboard the *Charlotte* around mid-December, he should be here by the end of January." He sighed.

"I wish to heaven by some miracle the *Charlotte* could have gotten under way earlier and reached Falmouth before the first of December. Now I shall have a fight on my hands trying to unload her when she does arrive."

"What do you mean, dear?" His mother put down her knitting and looked at him anxiously.

"When they met in Philadelphia in September the Continental Congress drew up a Nonimportation Agreement. It goes into effect December first against Great Britain, Ireland, and the British West Indies. The *Charlotte* will be carrying a cargo from Holland, but there will also be British goods aboard—woolens, mostly."

"And you cannot land them, sir?" Katharine asked incredulously.

"Not without a bribe or a fight. We shall see. The town voted some time back to observe a nonimportation agreement on tea. Now the Continental Congress is putting real teeth into an embargo, for all of the colonies have agreed to observe this Agreement. The hope, of course, is to bring England to her knees."

"Will it, sir?"

"It is a two-edged sword. Britain will suffer, naturally. Her manufacturers need colonial markets. But some of the merchant families here will be well-nigh ruined if they cannot sell their masts and lumber and fish."

"It is outrageous!" Mrs. Winter exclaimed hotly. "Who are these people to dictate to us? Republicans and levelers! How shall we live, pray? Without wool for our gowns, without needles and pins—why, your new suit is coming aboard the *Charlotte,* is it not?" With a worried frown she looked at her son. "The one you ordered your tailor in London to make up for you?"

"Yes." His face relaxed a moment in an indulgent smile. "But the suit, Mother, is the least of my worries. Perhaps you will have to spin again, my dear, and weave, too—go in homespun as the rebels swear they will before they'll buy a yard of English goods!"

"Never!" Mrs. Winter's dark eyes snapped as she spoke. "Not while there is an inch of good English wool to be had!"

"Perhaps I should learn to spin," Katharine said soberly, spreading her hands to the flames and looking at her fingers critically. "I can neither spin nor weave. I can knit, of course, but if it comes to homespun——"

"It will not, mark my words." The older woman interrupted. "Boston is hungry already, as well she should be." Her tone was that of a reproving parent. "She has brought starvation on herself listening to that rabble-rouser Samuel Adams! She is not alone in her rebellious tendencies. There has always been a refractory element here in Falmouth, too. Why, I well remember that in 1766, at the time of the Stamp Act, a mob marched to the Custom House and demanded the stamp papers which had arrived just that day from Halifax. After receiving them, they carried them through the town on the end of a pole and finally burned them!"

When she spoke again her tone was milder, almost

benign. "But you'll see; it will pass. In a little while this whole unhappy affair will blow over—like a summer storm." Taking up her knitting again, she gave a snort of disgust. "Bother! I've dropped a stitch! Katharine, can you find it for me?"

Obediently Katharine took up the knitting. Until the day of her death, no doubt, Mrs. Winter would be able to dismiss the irritating and the troublesome, the girl thought with a wry smile. Always there would be someone to place a footstool for her well-shod feet, always someone to search out the dropped stitch. In birth, in bearing, and in outlook she was quality, possessed of a placid assurance that within her small world all would forever be serene.

She herself had been born to such a world, the girl thought nostalgically as she bent her head in search of the lost stitch. A gracious place, her early home had sheltered the Leslie family for generations. There had been the London house, too. Perhaps because these were her most happy memories, her remembrance of them was most keen. In those early years her mother had been carefree, her father gay and charming. Later, everything had narrowed in a nightmare of smaller and shabbier houses, fewer servants, turned frocks; and most vivid and terrifying to a young child, her mother's drawn face and anxious eyes. Mercifully her mind had buried most of the rest. But the picture of her aunt, she realized, was coming into clearer focus. Now she saw the old woman's strictness as necessary for her own self-discipline, the unremitting instruction imperative in providing a tool Katharine could always employ.

It was fruitless to dream of herself as mistress of a home such as she had once known, Katharine reflected wistfully, especially in an England forbidden her. But it required little effort to imagine herself in a household such as this—the wife, perhaps, of an esteemed merchant, a man of substance, overseer of a comfortable and secure estate.

Finding the lost stitch, she worked it up to its proper place and returned the knitting. Mrs. Winter accepted it as her due. But her son sent Katharine a grateful smile and thanked her.

9}

She had almost forgotten how he looked, Katharine thought with a start, as she stood in the drawing room this January afternoon gazing up at Michael Edes. His lean face was burned by salt and winter winds almost to blackness. A new velvet ribbon caught back his hair, but his suit was the same old serge, she saw instantly, covering his body with the casual air of the long worn and comfortable. And his glance had not changed—candid, unaffected, it was as keen as a boy's. As he raised her fingers to his lips, her heart sang suddenly with the joy of seeing him again.

"I feared you might have changed," he said quietly, his eyes intent on hers. "But I see you have not. Your eyes are still as blue and deep as the January seas." Embarrassed at his own compliment, he laughed a little and stood off to survey her with the scrutiny of the physician. "One improvement I must remark on. At last, thank God, you have some flesh on your bones!"

She laughed, too, as she rose from her curtsy, her eyes darkening a moment in gentle mockery. "And you have acquired a new velvet ribbon!"

"Ah—you noticed. Mrs. Black assured me you would," he replied with a grin. "It is my one concession to fashion."

They moved to the fire where Edmund Winter stood. His mother sat in her usual chair. Annette was curled up in a corner of the small sofa, her attention entirely absorbed in a handsome fashion doll, elegantly gowned in the latest mode; a gift from her cousin, who had purchased this Paris beauty for her in London. Earlier in the day the family had gone to the wharf to welcome Michael aboard the *Charlotte*. Not wishing to intrude, Katharine had remained at home, waiting until now to offer her greeting.

Mrs. Winter spoke, gazing up at her nephew fondly. "What are your plans, Michael?"

"I hope, ma'am, to practice medicine. I have corresponded with Dr. Coffin, and I called on him a short while back. He assures me there is work enough here for two men."

His cousin sent him a shrewd look. "Will it be as profitable as your London practice?"

"I do not think it can be said that I have ever had a

really profitable practice," Michael said wryly, glancing at his worn cuffs. "But of course there are fortunes to be made in London, especially if one is willing to curry the favor of ancient widows and dyspeptic old lords."

"You might well have remained there perhaps."

"Except that everything I know—and admire—is here."

His cousin gave a short laugh. "You will find no sentiment among the rebels, believe me."

"The breach is fully as bad, then, as I have gathered these last few hours?"

"Worse." Edmund flung round impatiently. "To-morrow I shall be called before a town committee especially appointed to make sure none of my London cargo ever sees the light of day. This outrage condoned, nay, *ordered*, by the Continental Congress!"

"But if it works—this refusal to take British goods—" Michael spoke slowly, "if we succeed in forcing Parliament to reopen the port of Boston, to give back the rights granted by charter, surely——"

"*We!*" Edmund sent him a wrathful look. "In heaven's name, man, whose side are you on?"

Michael drew a long breath. "I don't yet fully know, Edmund," he said without rancor. "It seems to me there is something to be said on both sides."

"By God, I should like to hear you state the case for the rebels," his cousin said darkly.

Quickly the cordiality between the two men shrank to bitterness. Katharine sat silent. It was Mrs. Winter who spoke, shaking out her black gown as she rose from her chair.

"I must have my nap," she said in calm tones. "And you, dear," she addressed her son, "have much to do, I know, with a ship just in. Michael, perhaps Katharine will permit you to see some of Annette's work. She has improved."

In the schoolroom Annette drew out her drawings first and presented them proudly.

"Ah," Michael murmured appreciatively. "I recognize St. Paul's Church here in Middle Street. But what is this large white object in the background—a cloud going by?"

Annette shook her head. "It's a sea gull." Taking the painting from him, she perused it critically. "Perhaps it is a little large for a bird," she conceded doubtfully.

"Not at all!" Her cousin stoutly defended the painting. "Especially if he has been feasting on herring!"

"Would you care to see my book of sums?"

"Yes, indeed."

This consisted of four sheets of paper tied together at one edge with blue ribbon. Several exercises in arithmetic had been copied down in carefully executed figures. Michael studied each page before he returned it.

"I see that you have arrived at the correct answer in every case," he commented.

"Yes." Annette looked at Katharine. "And you did not tell me a single one, did you?" she exclaimed with pride.

Michael moved to the bookshelves. "What are you reading now?" he asked.

"A *Midsummer Night's Dream*. It is by William Shakespeare."

He smiled. "I believe I know it. And do you enjoy it?"

Annette nodded happily. "Oh, yes. Because Katharine and I read the parts aloud, and sometimes we act them out!"

Meeting hers, Michael's dark eyes smiled into Katharine's a moment, but when he spoke he addressed Annette.

"You approve my choice of governess, I take it?"

In answer Annette flung her arms around her teacher. Then, drawing away a little, she faced her cousin with sober eyes.

"But you must know that we work terribly hard," she said in earnest tones.

He laughed and rumpled her blond hair with a playful hand. "That is as it should be. Now I wonder, my sweet, if you would allow me five minutes of your teacher's time? I have something to discuss with her."

Annette gathered up the new doll and took herself off.

Michael turned to Katharine. "In one quarter, at least, you seem to be fully appreciated," he said with a smile. "Tell me, are you happy here in my cousin's household?"

"Oh, yes," she answered warmly. "Everyone has been most kind—your cousin especially."

"Edmund is a generous man, though sore pressed now by the stress of events." Moving a little closer, he lowered his voice. "I did not wish to mention it earlier, but you will be happy to learn that the turnkey Goss was not seriously harmed. The fall did little other than knock him senseless a few minutes."

"Thank God," she murmured gratefully. "I feared I might have killed him." Looking up into his face, she searched it with anxious eyes. "And you?"

"They questioned me, of course, for I am known in the prison, and Goss recalled that I had been your first visitor. But they were inclined to blame the gypsy woman."

For an instant the whole nightmare lived again in her mind, vivid and terrifying. Katharine shuddered.

He put a steadying hand on hers. "It is over now," he said firmly.

From his coat pocket he drew out a scrap of paper. "A week or two before I sailed I was at The Bell with a group of friends. The party got rather noisy, I fear, for we were seeing a colleague off to his first practice. One of the maids overheard my name and later drew me aside. She said she was Annie Moore, and that a seaman in from the West Indies had brought this message to her."

Recalling Mary's friend who worked in the tavern near Newgate, Katharine felt her heart tighten, and she took the paper with an unsteady hand. Carefully she smoothed the wrinkles until she could make out the words, all formed in large letters and one or two splotched with ink.

"*JAMAICA,*" she read slowly aloud. "*BILLY AND ME WEL—SERVINT TO GOOD MASTER— MARY.*" As she read it a second time and a third, the words blurred, but Mary and Billy were as sharp in her memory as if they stood before her eyes.

"I dared not reveal your whereabouts, but I tipped her generously, and I think we understood each other," the man beside her said quietly.

"Thank you," she whispered.

Staring down at the paper, she could imagine Mary, pen in hand, laboring over the letters—all capitals, since there had not been time to teach her others. How painstakingly she had formed the words, which were so carefully done, if imperfectly spelled. And how cheerfully triumphant she must have been when she had completed the message! Happiness at her friend's safety and gratitude at her good fortune swept her with such force that Katharine was suddenly close to tears.

She felt the doctor's eyes upon her, and looked up to find him regarding her anxiously.

"Surely this is all anyone could ask for her and the child?" he asked gently.

"Yes, oh, yes!" she agreed. Then regaining her composure, she smiled up at him. "It—it is not that I am sad," she stammered, trying to explain her incongruous behavior. "It is just that———"

"I know." Taking her arm, he led her across the room to the doorway. "Let us go and find Annette," he suggested, and she saw the twinkle in his dark eyes. "Before she pulls all her old dolls to pieces trying to fashion them into the latest Paris models!"

10

Except for Katharine, the schoolroom was deserted this February morning, for Annette was confined to her room with a cold. She had been quite content to take Michael's advice and remain in bed, happily aware that a morning free of lessons would give her ample time to study her dolls and plan new wardrobes for them.

Outside, snow fell in large, wet flakes, but within, everything was cozy. Close to the hearth, where a fire blazed, Katharine had drawn up a table and had laid out on it a large piece of green linen. The edges of the material had been damaged by sea water, but by cutting carefully she had secured enough for several book jackets. These she now fitted to the school texts, whose covers of heavy flowered paper were almost worn through. As she threaded her needle in preparation for sewing the first one into place, she was interrupted by Edmund Winter.

"Ah, Katharine." Newspapers in hand, her employer came into the room and stood by the fire. "You are wonderfully snug in here!"

Katharine smiled up at him. "I am indeed, sir."

"May I join you? I believe it is warmer here than anywhere else in the house this morning." He glanced at the woodbox and laughed. "Somehow Rome always sees that the schoolroom woodbox is stacked the highest!"

He sat down in an armchair, drew on his spectacles, and began to read the London papers which had arrived the day before by ship. In her early days in the household, Katharine had dreaded the advent of these papers, fearing always an allusion to herself. But her employer paid scant attention to anything other than political news, she had discovered with relief.

"The same old arguments! Why doesn't His Majesty's Government realize that the only way to subdue the rebels is to use the rod unsparingly?" He threw down the papers and turned to her. "You know, of course, that the Town Committee graciously permitted me to land my cargo from the *Charlotte*," he added satirically.

"Yes, sir." She nodded, knowing that the merchant had been allowed to land his English goods and store them in his warehouse. There, by decree of Congress, they must remain.

"I could sell the wool, of course," he went on bitterly. "But the Committee would allow me only enough to meet the original cost. Any profit would go to the relief of the poor in Boston." His clenched fist came down on the arm of the chair with a resounding slap. "Rather than pay money to Sam Adams and his crew of cutthroats, I'll see the bales rot first!"

To bury fine English wool, foreign silks, and brocades in the musty dampness of a warehouse, simply because they had been purchased through English merchants, seemed to Katharine an outrage.

"What of your own suit, sir, the one your tailor in London made up for you?' she asked in sympathy.

"Ah." The expression of his face changed. "I smuggled it ashore! True, I split the seams of my old coat cramming it over the new one, but by heaven it was worth it! I have managed to smuggle one or two other things home, too," he said with a little smile of triumph. "None of us need go in rags or homespun yet!"

Would there be handsome materials for Annette and perhaps for herself? With a happy sense of anticipation, Katharine returned to her sewing. Perhaps her employer would make her a gift of new material as he had of the rose wool for the gown she was now wearing. But if he did not, she herself could afford to buy stuff for another gown. Only a few days back her quarterly wage had been paid in good British gold.

She came back to the subject. "Is there no way the King's men can retaliate against these rebel measures, sir?"

"Let us give the devils their due," Edmund responded dryly. "The rebels are far better organized than we are. They saw to that early through their Committees of Correspondence. If we who are loyal would organize, we might accomplish something! But while we remain irresolute, the rebels gain strength. Why, last month Falmouth citizens assessed themselves eighty pounds for gunpowder. Gunpowder—raised by rebels in the King's province! I tremble to think what use they may make of it! And fifty-one cords of wood have been sent from Falmouth to Boston to keep the hotheads there from freezing."

He adjusted his wig, a gesture always indicative of irritation, she had learned, and spoke more calmly. "You are a good listener, Katharine," he said in compliment, and she blushed in pleasure as he returned to the papers.

In the past few weeks the relationship between them had subtly changed. Lately they had attained somehow an easier cordiality, initiated by Edmund. If she had not patently encouraged this new intimacy, she had most certainly done nothing to discourage it, Katharine admitted honestly. How much did it mean? Beneath her lashes, she studied her employer. From his carefully brushed wig to his silver-buckled shoes, everything about him bespoke elegance and substance. And her own present comfort—the gown she wore, the food she enjoyed, the very warmth of this room—all were a part of his bounty. Recalling the lifeless chill of Newgate, the decayed and rotten food, Goss with his thick fingers and calculating eyes, Katharine suppressed a shudder. How had she ever endured such an existence? At the time the nightmare had been real enough, but now it seemed an awful dream, a fantasy.

As she glanced out into the storm of snow, she felt the schoolroom fire warm at her back, and as her gaze returned to the room, it lingered an instant on her new gown, rosy-red in the glow of the flames. A sense of well-being stole over her, so all-pervading and familiar, that recognizing its significance, Katharine felt a shock of dismay. The shelter and comfort provided here with such munificence she no longer regarded as luxuries, she realized, but as necessities to her happiness. What if she were forced to forego them? Could she? *Need she?*

She looked back to the fire and found Edmund's eyes upon her.

"A penny for your thoughts," he suggested with a smile.

For a moment she considered telling him of Newgate. Was she not innocent? But what proof could she offer? By a King's magistrate she had been branded a thief. And honesty could demand a bitter price, as she had learned to her sorrow. She had been honest with herself in refusing to compromise her good name. And Newgate had been her reward. No, she would not risk an explanation or confession, at least not yet, she decided, letting the impulse die.

Her employer seemed not to notice her silence. Crossing to the table, he took up a text, now neatly covered in its sheath of protective linen. Carefully he inspected her work.

"No one else has ever taken such an interest," he said quietly. "I am in your debt."

"Oh, no, sir," she murmured, conscious of his steady gaze and the warm approval in his look. "I am happy to be of service."

In the next instant a shadow crossed the doorway, and Michael drew up abruptly on the threshold. His quick glance swept from Edmund to Katharine.

"I beg your pardon!" His tone and demeanor became stiffly formal as he handed a note to the older man. "Forgive me for intruding, cousin, but Captain Pagan begs a reply to this within the hour."

Edmund broke the seal, perused the note, then thrust it aside irritably. "More to do with these new rebel laws and orders," he muttered. Moving to the desk, he sat down heavily, drew out a sheet of paper and picked up a pen. He examined the point critically a moment before he flung it down with an exclamation of disgust.

Katharine jumped up. "Let me mend it for you, sir," she offered quickly. Going to the desk, she drew out a small penknife from one of the pigeonholes. Carefully she pared the quill and returned it to him.

He touched the sharpened point to his finger tip.

"Ah, much better indeed! Thank you, Katharine. What a blessing you are," he said gratefully, opening the ink-pot and dipping the quill in.

Looking up, she saw Michael's glance resting on her, a gleam of amusement in his dark eyes. Under that long gaze she felt her face flame, and then was lost in fury at herself. There was no cause to blush. The act had been innocent of guile. How dare he! Turning her back on him, she took her place at the table and again resumed her work. Yet she was aware, whether she admitted it or not, that her quick service had done her no harm in her employer's eyes.

By Sunday Annette had recovered, and, as usual, accompanied the family to church. Almost without exception the Tories of Falmouth worshipped at St. Paul's in Middle Street. In pleasant weather the Winter family walked the short distance, but this morning was cold and blustery with a threat of snow. With the coachman Sam and a boy on the driver's seat, the sleigh carried Mrs. Winter, Annette, and Katharine. Edmund and Michael walked.

Katharine found herself seated in the Winter pew between Michael and her pupil. Annette always fidgeted, for she was impatient at best and the service was long. Today the sermon was of interminable length, Katharine reflected with a sigh, the Reverend Wiswall seemingly inspired.

Before he had taken his place with the other servants at the back of the church, Sam had placed foot warmers at each lady's feet. But the coals had gradually burned out, and wriggle her toes as she would, Katharine could not keep them warm. Annette suddenly sneezed, and her teacher cast her an anxious look.

"It's the scent Madame Cavendish uses," her pupil whispered, sending a dark glance at the stylish young widow seated in the pew directly in front of them. "It tickles my nose."

Her teacher nodded and put up an admonishing finger. Only a few minutes after their own arrival, Mr. Dunmore, his wife, and their guest had swept into the Dunmore pew. From head to foot Pamela Cavendish was swathed in black, but somehow the somber hue did not diminish the flash of her hazel eye nor the flame of her auburn hair. And the scent that had touched off in Annette an explosive sneeze had mercilessly teased Katharine to vain dreams far removed from godly matters. The young widow's plight should have moved her to pity, she thought with a twinge of guilt. Even a large fortune could hardly compensate for a husband lost at sea after only six months of marriage, and this tragedy had been compounded by the villainy of the rebels who had driven her and her father, a royal judge, out of their home in Milton. Yet the waving jet ostrich plumes of her bonnet, and her rich cloak lined in some warm, dark fur, evoked in Katharine only an envious appraisal, intensified by a convulsive shiver brought on by the frigid atmosphere of the church.

While Annette squirmed on her one side, Michael was unusually quiet on her other, Katharine realized as the sermon wore relentlessly on. For the past ten days the young doctor had been up night and day, administering to young and old stricken with a sore throat that had reached almost epidemic proportions. Now, glancing at him from beneath the brim of her bonnet, she saw with dismay that his eyes were closed and his dark head bent slightly forward. Before the verger's fur-tipped rod could touch his ear, or a personal reprimand from the pulpit embarrass him, Katharine put a gentle hand on his arm.

"Wake up," she whispered.

His eyes flicked open, and he glanced down at her, blinking. Then he smiled, and she felt the grateful pressure of his fingers on her own an instant before she withdrew them.

When they assembled a half hour later outside the church, they found that snow had begun to fall.

Immediately Mrs. Winter took Mrs. Dunmore and her handsome guest under her protection. "Of course, Isabella, if you have no carriage here, you must ride with us," she insisted. "We shall be a little crowded, but Edmund and Robert can walk. And Michael will take care of Katharine. She will not mind the walk, I am sure."

Since every snowflake was a threat to the ladies' ribbons and plumes, they got into the sleigh quickly and huddled beneath the fur robes. Sam touched the whip to the horses and they pulled away. With chilled fingers Katharine drew the hood of her scarlet cloak up over her new velvet bonnet and shoved her feet more resolutely into her clogs.

"Have you nothing for your feet but those inadequate pattens?" Michael demanded with a frown.

She shook her head, not trusting herself to speak. The casual snub, bestowed quite unwittingly by Mrs. Winter, had fanned the flame of her resentment, already kindled in church by the young widow's elegance and poise. To be relegated to the roadway was degrading enough, Katharine thought rebelliously, but to be thrust there under the cool eye of Pamela Cavendish was more than she could bear.

"Oh, if only I were my own mistress!" she burst out passionately, stumbling in her anger as she took a step on the icy road and almost falling.

Michael caught her up. "My aunt meant no harm," he said quickly. "It is just that——"

"It is just that she regards me as a servant," Katharine interposed coldly.

He tucked her gloved hand more firmly within his arm. "Does it matter so much?"

"Of course it matters!" Her blue eyes blazed into his. "Do you suppose that I enjoy such treatment? That I want to spend all of my days at someone's beck and call? I—I should like to be established in a home of my own!" she cried with an exasperation that came close to tears.

He laughed. "So should we all." His eyes, intent on her face, suddenly softened. "Be patient a little longer, Katharine," he counseled, and then his voice lightened and she detected a hint of laughter in it. "What are you now? All of seventeen?"

But today Katharine could not respond to this light note. To envy the young widow was, she knew, irrational and unbecoming; she was even a little ashamed of herself. But Michael's casual disregard for her feelings only served to draw him within the orbit of her anger. Even Michael did not appreciate her position, she saw, as they picked their way among the icy ruts. Neither mistress nor servant, a governess dwelt in a dubious half-world from whence she could look either up or down. Since it was clearly impossible to imagine herself among the servants, there was only one choice, she reflected, feeling her resolve harden as the bitter Maine wind cut beneath her cloak. She would look up.

11

When Annette could play on the harpsichord two of
her grandmother's favorite hymns, *O God, Our Help
in Ages Past* and *While Shepherds Watched Their
Flocks by Night*, with neither a hesitation nor a false
note, her father declared a half holiday. Annette chose
to spend the winter morning sleighing with her teacher.

Tucked in the sleigh, cozy beneath a bearskin robe,
her feet shod in snug deerskin boots that Michael had
presented only the day before, Katharine rejoiced in the
brilliant sunshine, the frosty air, and the jingling of the
bells as she and Annette were driven up King Street.
To protect her complexion Annette wore a new face
mask of black velvet, recommended by her grandmother,
but she discarded it almost at once, declaring the slits

for the eyes were too narrow to allow her to see properly.

"King Street is my favorite street," she mused contentedly, caressing her bare cheek with a small muff of soft beaver. "What is yours, Katharine?"

"Oh, the same, to be sure!" Katharine agreed happily, surveying with a light heart the handsome houses sparkling in snow and sunlight.

At the top of King Street they turned into Back Street, and a moment later Annette tugged at her teacher's arm.

"Look, there is Mrs. Greele's tavern. You remember it." She pointed to a long, low building, and Katharine recalled the day of Sheriff Tyng's "humbling," and the crowd of men pressing into the tavern afterward. Annette's voice dropped to a whisper. "It's a favorite meeting place for the rebels. Father never goes there, but Michael does."

"Are you sure?"

"Yes. They all drink flip and talk politics half the night."

Why must Michael demean himself by associating with the rebels in this low fashion? the older girl wondered in annoyance.

In this section of Back Street there were a number of good-sized dwellings, one or two impressive, but as they advanced along the road the houses grew smaller and less numerous. On their left now a windmill stood out above the snow-covered fields, its sails turning steadily under the winter wind. Further along they came upon a solitary house, small and snug, set close to the road. In the icy dooryard a young woman, her ragged shawl flapping from her shoulders, struggled to lower a well sweep into a well. Her hands were red and raw from the cold, and her face, dark-eyed and haggard, staring out at them, resembled Mary Fletcher's, Katharine saw, feeling a sudden, sharp pity.

Annette's voice was half lost in her muff as she snuggled it against her cheek. "*She* is certainly not one of *us!*" she murmured. "Did you see her shawl?"

"You must not despise her simply because she is poor!" Katharine exclaimed sharply, shocked at her pupil's smug tone.

"Oh, I do not despise her!" Annette's brows flew up in genuine astonishment. "Since we are not even acquainted, how could I?"

The sleigh jingled on, its bells gay on the frosty air. It was foolish to let the casual words of a child mar the day, Katharine thought, vexed that she could not dismiss the incident from her mind. In their six months together she had brought the younger girl to a sense of discipline and a measure of accomplishment far beyond that imposed by any other teacher, she was sure. Yet if her pupil were to become a woman with neither compassion nor understanding, as a teacher she herself could hardly be called a success. Was Annette's callous view a reflection of her own? In attaining a measure of security had she herself begun to lose her sense of charity for those less fortunate? Her reaction to the rebels was one of complete outrage, she admitted, tempered by no tolerance whatever. Yet, they *were* rebels! Still, she wondered uneasily, would she have inveighed as strongly against them from a Newgate cell a year ago?

Now on their right the Meeting House of the First Parish came into view. Beside the house stood a handsome parsonage.

"Dr. Deane lives there." Annette pointed. "He is a rebel, too, even though he is a man of God."

Katharine smiled, and trying to recapture the earlier mood, caught up the hand of her pupil in an affectionate squeeze. "You are better than a gazette! I see now why your mind is so seldom on your lessons! It is too fully occupied with town affairs," she chided lightly.

When they reached Haymarket Square, Sam guided the horses into Middle Street. Here, on the downgrade, the sleigh sped over the snow, sending up a biting spray from the runners. Katharine was lost to every feeling except the intoxication induced by speed and wind.

"It's as if we were flying!" she gasped happily, her breath blown back in her throat, her cheeks stinging under the wind.

But the pace was short-lived, for opposite St. Paul's Church Sam was suddenly forced to pull up to make way for a heavy sledge drawn by oxen. When the team was safely past, he clucked to the horses and they moved on again. It was at this moment that a snowball hit the old coachman squarely in the face. With a groan he flung up a hand to his cheek and the reins went slack.

"Sam!" Shocked into action, Katharine was on her feet, leaning forward. "Are you hurt?"

Sam gathered up the reins and drew to a halt. "No, ma'am," he said shakily. "Just—just blinded for a minute." As he took the handkerchief she offered to wipe away the snow, another ball struck him.

"*Tory! Tory! Slave and Tory!*" The taunt came sharp and derisive from the street.

Outraged, the girl turned to see two boys doubled up with laughter at their prank, neither one aware of the small fury bearing down on them that was Annette.

"Annette!" She leaped from the sleigh and ran toward the group. But she was not in time to prevent Annette's hurling a handful of snow into one grinning, unsuspecting face.

"*Rebel! Rebel! Scum and rebel!*" Annette shrilled wrathfully, mimicking their own cry.

"*Annette!*"

"They hit Sam!" Annette's voice broke on a sob as she pointed to the boys now racing away. "How dare they do it!"

"Come and get back into the sleigh," Katharine said quietly, striving for a calm she did not feel.

As they moved on she offered no word of reproach, for she knew that Annette's retaliation had sprung from a loyalty and love too deep to be censured. She need have no misgivings about Annette, she saw in gratitude. Despite the quick and callous words on Back Street, her heart was warm and generous. Beneath the fur robe she held the trembling figure close.

But where would it end? she wondered, as Sam drove them into King Street and deposited them at their own door. If even the children were caught up in the bitter struggle between rebel and Tory—where would it end?

That night she could not sleep. As soon as the fire was out, the room seemed to shrink to a small, black cave, darkly cold. From the northeast the wind struck the windows in spiteful gusts, hurling snow and ice in the opening blows of a blizzard. Shivering, she tucked up her toes in the folds of her nightgown and burrowed again in the depths of the mattress. But tonight even the goose down failed her, and finally, in search of another warm brick for her bed, she crept down to the kitchen, her long woolen dressing gown murmuring over the back stairs.

The light of her candle was greeted by another, and she saw Michael in shirt and breeches, tall in the shadows, holding his dripping cloak to the fire.

"Michael," she whispered. Startled to find him here at this hour, she turned to go back.

"Don't go." Dropping the cloak over a chair, he came toward her. "Give me a hand with my boots, will you?"

He sat down on the fireside bench and thrust out his feet. Katharine knelt, feeling the boots sodden and slippery in her hands. Since she applied no great pressure as she tried to ease one off, she was startled when Michael winced and uttered a half-stifled groan.

"What is it?" she exclaimed anxiously.

His smile was rueful. "My leg. It's been giving me a devil of a time these last hours."

She had almost forgotten the long convalescence of a year ago. Surely the leg should be strong by now? A little frown gathered between her brows.

"Don't look so concerned, I beg," he said lightly. "I feel it only when I'm tired. And it's been a long day." He bent down. "Here, let me help."

Together they worked off the boots.

"My grateful thanks, ma'am." He gave her a smile, and then swung round to the fire, rubbing his hands before the blaze. "I walked the last two miles, and it's no weather for it. We were a fine pair, Blackie and I. The horse limping—God knows what went wrong with his knee—and I hobbled in these damn boots."

"What happened?" she asked, moving closer to the fire.

"John Bates came for me earlier today. The midwife sent him, for she needed help." A wry grin twisted his mouth. "She did certainly, but so did I. Between us we delivered twin sons, two boys as hale and hearty as you'll ever see."

"And Mrs. Bates?"

"This was her third lying-in. And the other two children are girls."

Katharine smiled with him. "Then she, too, is happy."

"But I am exhausted." He gave an exaggerated sigh and looked at her quizzically. "Tell me, my lovely lady, did you descend from the upper regions to brew me a cup of my cousin's contraband tea?"

With a laugh, she turned her back on him and stretched her hands to the flames. "That was not my original intention, sir. But you have the kettle on the hob, I see."

"It was my first thought." He sent her a more searching look. "Why are you here, if I may ask?"

"I couldn't get warm," she said with a shiver, hearing even now the bleak wind at her windows.

"It's blowing up a blizzard. Sit here." He moved to the end of the bench. "There's plenty of room beside me."

"I—I can't stay." Suddenly she was aware of her robe and slippers, and the two long braids down her back.

"Please—" His eyes mocked her. "At two o'clock in the morning, must you be genteel?"

"Let me make the tea first."

"Very well. And while you do, tell me about the day's events."

She warmed the pot, put in a generous measure of the precious tea, poured boiling water over it, and meanwhile related Annette's encounter.

"Ah—" He laughed softly as she finished. "If all those loyal to the King had half her spirit, the rebel cause would die a quick death."

Katharine placed the teapot on the hearth, got two

cups and put them beside it. Then she took her place on the bench again and looked squarely into his face.

"Are you a rebel, Michael?"

His eyes met hers in a long, straight look. "I see something in both sides," he said slowly, "and that is my dilemma. God knows I deplore the tactics of Sam Adams, the tar and the feathers of the mob, the rabble-rousing. But neither do I believe that Parliament—no matter what the provocation—can revoke the rights given us by charter. And that is what they have done."

"Surely it will end soon?"

"I suppose it must. All of the strength, except the strength of spirit and endeavor, is with the King. He has the money, the power, and the troops."

"Then why doesn't he *do* something?" she demanded impatiently. "Why must we be subjected to these hot-heads? They are spoiling everything. There is no comfort, no security for any of us!"

"There is none for the rebels either, my little Tory." His voice was dry. Leaning down he gave an appreciative sniff. "Do you think the tea is ready?"

She poured a cup for him and one for herself.

Now, over the cup, he looked at her intently, his dark eyes sober. " 'Comfort and security,' you said," he repeated. "Is that what you are looking for, Katharine?"

Something in his tone set her instantly on guard. "Is it not the dream of every woman?" she countered swiftly. "A home, a family? If they can be had in comfort—even luxury—is that wrong?"

"Not if you include the other requisites."

"What other requisites?"

"Mutual esteem—love."

Katharine answered with a laugh that was half amusement, half mockery. "One cannot have everything," she said lightly. "Bread and butter come first. Newgate taught me that."

He was silent, and she went on in swift vindication of her point.

"Here"—putting down her cup, she spread her hands wide—"here in Falmouth I believed at first that everything was safe, secure. The house, the servants, the horses, the carriage—all of your cousin's possessions bespeak a certain position, a certain stability. The food is good, the house is warm, the clothes are beautiful—" She broke off, aware of the wistful note that had crept into her voice. Meeting his, her eyes darkened in sudden anger. "But below it all is the constant threat of the rebels! They muster and march. They bully and abuse. They threaten everything and everyone! How I have come to hate them!"

He put down his cup and turned to her abruptly. "Have you considered their side? That they risk everything you name, nay, their very lives, too, in their fight to secure the rights of freeborn Englishmen?"

"*I do not care about their side!*" Katharine cried ruthlessly, flinging out the words in a paroxysm of wrath, astonished at the depth of her passion.

For a long moment he measured her. "I see that I was

wrong in my estimate of you," he said at last. "You are changed indeed."

"How do you mean?" she asked quickly.

"In Newgate you fought for Mary and her child. You were bitter against the tyranny of Goss—not so much for yourself as for them." He came to his feet and swung round on her. When he spoke, his voice was as biting as the winter wind. "Now you consider only your own skin," he said coldly.

The words stung, and Katharine winced under them. Then she stiffened in defiance, swept by a flooding anger at his presuming to judge her.

He spoke again. "I am aware that you mend my cousin's pens, rebind his books, and bestow flattering attention on his political views." There was a sardonic edge to Michael's voice. "Tell me, if you please, just how *he* fits into your plans?"

Her cheeks flamed. Always he anticipated her!

"So." He nodded. "I fear you are not only mercenary, my sweet. You are scheming as well."

"I am not!" On her feet she faced him in swift denial.

"Are you not? You speak of houses and horses and carriages!" His voice was scathing in its contempt, and Katharine felt as if he flayed her with the words. Then his tone softened a little. "Oh, I can understand your longing for security. You saw the impotence of poverty in prison, and the power of money." Sharpening again, his voice grew harsh, and the look he gave her was long and hard. "But is that *all* you have seen? What of integrity? Have you told Edmund of Newgate?"

"No," she whispered.

"Do you love him?"

"Not—not as you mean."

"Then you cheat him."

Humiliated by the truth he had so relentlessly wrenched from her, she struck back wrathfully.

"Who are you to judge me? Are you not a rebel—or close to one—in your cousin's household? At least I am loyal. As to devotion, affection—the question has not arisen." She flung up her head, her eyes blazing into his. "And what right have you to counsel me on the subject?"

"None, God knows," he said with a brittle laugh.

Forgetful of her errand now, desiring only to escape his merciless glance and probing questions, Katharine snatched up her candle, seeing its flame waver in her shaking hand.

"Allow me." Taking it from her, Michael led her up the shadowy stairway, the silence falling heavy and thick between them. He opened the door of her chamber, and as he set the candle on the table, she saw his face, dark and withdrawn—an expression new and frightening to her. Like a child, she thought painfully, she had lashed out at his words—as if blatant and furious denial made them any less the truth.

"Please," she whispered, putting out a hand. "Must we part in anger?"

At first she thought he had not heard. Then he caught up her hands in his own and looked at her searchingly.

"A man deserves honesty, Katharine," he said quietly. "Be honest with Edmund in all things—and with yourself." His fingers relaxed on hers, and he bowed in good night.

12

In March, Captain Samuel Coulson, a resident of King Street and a prominent Tory, asked permission of the town committee to land rigging, sails, and stores purchased in England to outfit a mast ship he was building at a Falmouth wharf. When the ship was outfitted, his intention was to load her with the tall pine masts of Maine and carry them to England. The town committee refused his request. Outraged, Captain Coulson sailed to Boston, procured the help of the Royal Navy, and a few days later arrived in Casco Bay escorted by His Majesty's Ship *Canseaux*. Under her guns, in open defiance of the terms of the Nonimportation Agreement, boycotting British goods, he began to land his English stores.

Captain Coulson's sturdy defiance gave new heart to the Tory merchants of Falmouth. This March afternoon Edmund Winter was plainly exultant. Except Annette, who was attending a birthday party, the family had dined together as usual, though Michael's presence at the main meal of the day was a rarity. Too often his country patients claimed him, and he seldom partook of Polly's delicious dinners. Today's baked halibut and creamed potatoes, cold ham and buttered eggs, fresh bread and Dutch cheese, jam tartlets and tea, had found him in hearty appetite.

Retiring to the drawing room as soon as the meal was finished, the group gathered around the fire, Mrs. Winter claiming her favorite chair, Katharine the velvet hassock. Edmund Winter, elegant in the brilliant silk of a new plum-colored suit, continued to rejoice in the welcome arrival of Samuel Coulson and the *Canseaux*.

"If Coulson can defy the town government and the Association, we all have a chance," he said with a little crow of triumph, rubbing his hands happily before the blaze.

"I understand Captain Coulson is having trouble getting men to rig the new ship for him," Michael replied quietly in answer to his cousin's comment.

"True, but Captain Mowat has ordered a few marines from the *Canseaux* to pick up some of the stragglers and idlers off the wharves, I'm told." The older man gave a deep-throated chuckle. "And believe me, any man impressed into His Majesty's service works—or feels the lash on his back!"

Mrs. Winter looked up from the damask napkin she was hemming. "It is certainly time someone stood up to these irresponsible rebels," she agreed. "Why, when I think of all that beautiful material of yours lying useless in that warehouse—" She sighed, and took up her needle again.

"Do you believe, then, that this may be the end of the trouble?" Raising her eyes from her knitting, Katharine looked at Michael.

"I certainly do not!" he replied in firm tones. "In fact, I consider it a great mistake for Coulson to have come here under the guns of a warship."

"Mistake!" Edmund flung round on him, the veins of his face thickening in anger. "It is full time we had more such 'mistakes' then! Great heaven! Who is to put this rabble in its place, if not the King's fleet?" With an irritable nod he turned to Rome, who had appeared in the doorway. "Well, Rome?"

"There is a gentleman asking for Doctor Edes, sir. He is waiting at the back door, sir."

"Michael, why the devil do all your patients choose the back door?" Edmund badgered.

The younger man sent a cool and merciless eye over his relative's finery. "Perhaps they are overwhelmed by your grandeur, dear cousin," he replied ironically. With a bow to his aunt and Katharine, he withdrew.

Mrs. Winter sighed and put down her needle. "It is

no laughing matter, this medical practice of his. Last month he deeply offended Isabella Dunmore." She turned to Katharine. "You recall the night of the February blizzard?"

"Yes, ma'am." The girl nodded. The memory of her quarrel with Michael still burned in her mind like a brand in the wind.

"Well, Isabella summoned Michael that day, for she was feeling quite ill. And Michael told her in no uncertain terms that in his opinion her headache was nothing but the vapors, and recommended a lighter diet and more exercise! Isabella is not accustomed to such brusque advice, and she was quite put out." Her tone sharpened to exasperation. "He seemed willing enough to rush off later in the day to assist at the birth of those Bates babies. Everyone knows John Bates. Michael will be lucky if he ever sees a shilling from *him!*"

"I must say he meets his board and room here punctiliously enough," her son spoke up in Michael's defense. "I confess there are times I feel guilty taking the sum he insists on. After all, he misses half his meals. But I suppose he has a backlog of savings from his London days."

"Not a penny, I'll wager." His mother looked up again. "Or surely he would buy himself another coat? I have searched his closet—after all, I *am* his aunt! And I could find only one other suit, the black silk. And if Annette had not made him that new linen shirt under Katharine's able guidance, there is not the least doubt in my mind that Michael would still be wearing the old one!"

"You mean that the black silk and the suit he wears on his back make up the full extent of his wardrobe?" Edmund's look was one of blank astonishment. Then he shrugged. "Oh, well, he dropped a lot at cards, I dare say. Every young blade plays at cards nowadays, and London is a hotbed of gambling."

Katharine lifted her head. To brand Michael a gambler—how unjust! Now was the time to speak of his generosity, of his munificent gifts to her in prison. She lay down her knitting and drew breath.

But Mrs. Winter spoke first. "No," she said with a slight frown, "I do not think Michael is a gambler. From something he let slip, I imagine he may have helped some of the prisoners in Newgate."

"In Newgate?" Her son sent her an incredulous glance. "Why in heaven's name would he waste his gold on the thieves and felons of Newgate?"

"Michael is generous to a fault." She looked up, meeting her son's astounded gaze. "And surely some of the prisoners are deserving of help?"

"In Newgate? Very few, madam, I assure you. The King's justice may be harsh, but it *is* just." Edmund's tone was coldly reproving. "Who is Michael to temper the decrees of the courts? Every thief, of course, cries out his innocence, but that is no excuse to soften the punishment!" The lines of his mouth drew sharply stern in judgment.

Trying to control the tremor of her hands, Katharine

took up her knitting again. Now she dared not reveal the full truth; it was too damning to herself. Though her heart beat hotly in Michael's defense, she could offer little more than a compromise.

"There—there was the money for my passage," she stammered.

Edmund turned to her. "I offered to pay him for that," he said graciously, "since you crossed in one of my ships and became a member of my household. But Michael wouldn't hear of any payment. He practically threw the money in my face!" His tone softened a little. "Perhaps because he made his home with us for so many years after the death of his parents, he feels that he must now be as independent as possible. But there is no need for him to be so sensitive. His father left enough to educate him, and Michael has always carried his own weight."

With a shrug her employer dismissed the subject, and came to stand beside her—a rich, imposing figure, casting a substantial shadow across her work. "How does the shawl progress?" he asked with a friendly smile.

Katharine spread the shawl, made of sapphire-blue yarn Edmund had presented to her a few weeks back, over the lap of her rose gown.

"It is going to be beautiful, as you can see," she murmured.

"It matches your eyes," he answered in a low tone. "A handsome shade of blue."

She blushed and began to knit again in embarrassed concentration.

Mrs. Winter spoke. "In your opinion, Katharine, is Annette progressing as well as ever?"

Welcoming the diversion, Katharine turned quickly to the older woman. "I am pleased with the work Annette has done, ma'am," she said slowly, "but I must confess that recently we have not progressed as much as I could hope. Town affairs are so—so turbulent, the Royal Marines of the *Canseaux* are sometimes abroad in the streets——"

"The little minx! Of course the uniforms attract her!" Her father's tone was indulgent. "But you have done remarkably well with her, nonetheless," he said more seriously. "Why, now she can even sew a little!"

"She would make a shirt for Michael if it were fashioned out of nettles!" his mother said tartly.

"True. But let us give her credit for making such a fine one out of linen," her son retorted with a laugh.

Katharine gathered up the shawl and rose. "If you will excuse me, ma'am, sir—I promised Annette that I would call for her at the Dunmores' before the party ended so that I might see Betsy's birthday gifts."

"Of course." Mrs. Winter nodded in dismissal.

"And I must return to the wharf." Edmund bowed to his mother and accompanied Katharine into the hallway. "May I escort you as far as the Dunmores'?" he asked.

"You are very kind, sir." She gave him a ready smile. "But surely it is out of your way?"

"A little, perhaps. But the day is fine, and I am in no great haste."

He helped her into her scarlet cloak, and while she stepped into her pattens, he drew on his own greatcoat.

Outside they found the March wind blustery, but the sun gave a feeble warmth that was a promise of spring. And the dirt road was beginning to yield its frost, Katharine saw in distaste, carefully stepping across the muddy ruts.

"I fancy this party will give the rebels one more cause for criticism," Edmund mused, as he guided her to drier ground.

"A child's birthday party?" she asked incredulously.

"Among the resolutions adopted by Congress last October was one discouraging entertainments." He gave a slight chuckle. "Well, the same resolution also frowns on mourning clothes, except a black crepe band or ribbon for gentlemen, and a ribbon or necklace for ladies. I fancy the Widow Cavendish must have caused quite a stir—arriving here in her sweeping black silks and plumes—all quite obviously new, and elegant into the bargain!"

They were in upper King Street now, and the walking had improved somewhat. Katharine took her gaze from the road long enough to meet her employer's keen blue eyes.

"Surely, sir, no one takes these Congressional resolutions seriously," she protested.

"They are taken very seriously," he answered soberly. "It is a mistake to suppose that the rebels do not mean every word of what they say."

In another moment he had unlatched the gate to the Dunmore house, and she was crunching the beach pebbles of the walk beneath her pattens. At the door he banged the knocker, and while they waited for a servant to admit her, Edmund took her hand and bowed over it.

"A pleasant walk, though not nearly long enough," he said gallantly.

"I enjoyed it, too," Katharine murmured, dipping in a curtsy as the door swung wide.

Inside, a servant took her cloak and pattens and led her at once to the drawing room where the hushed silence and rigid postures of the guests proclaimed a game of blindman's buff in progress. The older girl stood on the threshold and watched with a smile as a blindfolded guest appraised Annette, running exploring fingers over her face, the neck of her gown, then touching her hair, sweeping down its full length to her waist.

"Annette!" she exclaimed in triumph, peeling off the blindfold. The two girls fell into each other's arms in a paroxysm of giggles.

"But how did you know it was me?" Annette demanded.

"Your hair! Everyone's is long, but yours is so thick!"

Annette claimed her teacher and led her to the hall

where neatly arranged on a table were Betsy's gifts: two reticules, one of embroidered silk, the other of crimson velvet; a tortoise-shell comb; two lawn hand-kerchiefs trimmed with lace; several yards of pale blue ribbon; a pair of gloves; and a fan whose parchment, when opened up, displayed a pastoral scene of shepherds and shepherdesses.

"She likes my fan the best," Annette whispered. "I knew she would! Though her Mamma says she may not carry it beyond the house."

There had been much discussion over the appropriateness of such a gift to a girl of eleven. Some time back Annette had begged of her grandmother a fan considered by the widow too gaudy for her own use. Betsy Dunmore, as well as Katharine, had watched Annette's guileless blue eyes peer over the green trees and puffy clouds of the open fan, or the small hand vigorously fluttering shepherds and sheep. But whereas her teacher had suffered no emotion other than suppressed amusement at this innocent pastime, her friend had coveted the fan with such anguish that she had begged it as a gift. Today Annette had graciously bestowed it on her as a birthday offering.

They made their farewells and returned to the street, Annette happily enumerating the number of ices and cakes she had consumed, and confessing as they approached their own door that perhaps the slight discomfort she now felt might well be from a surfeit of ginger cookies.

13

Day after day, like a belligerent watchdog, His Majesty's Ship *Canseaux* guarded Falmouth, and under the protection of her guns, Captain Coulson outfitted his new mast ship with the naval stores purchased in England.

Though they could do little, there were angry mutterings by many townsmen. Katharine was aware of the disgruntled mood this April day, as she walked to Mrs. Mosely's shop on Fore Street, accompanied by Annette.

"People are staring at us," Annette murmured, drawing her wool cape closer.

"Hold your head high and look straight ahead," the older girl instructed quietly. She lifted her own shoulders beneath her scarlet cloak.

The Widow Mosely offered groceries, English and

West Indian goods, and a selection of laces, ribbons, gloves, mitts, fringe, and other accessories. But her small stock was already badly depleted; for the ladies of the town, Loyalist and rebel alike, had begun to quietly buy up whatever goods they could afford.

"Are there no white gloves to be had?" Annette, always fully aware of the necessities for her own wardrobe, looked about the almost empty shelves impatiently.

"There are two or three pairs left, miss." From a drawer beneath the counter the widow selected several pairs and put them out for Annette's inspection.

"But nothing in my size," the girl mourned. She held up a pair. "These might fit you, Katharine."

They were a perfect fit and Katharine bought them, eager to secure them while they were still to be had.

But her real reason for this visit to Mrs. Mosely's shop was to purchase some fine serge. She was determined to make Michael the gift of a coat. The conversation with Edmund and his mother had sharpened her sense of obligation to him. Acutely aware now of his threadbare wardrobe, and increasingly ashamed of her tardy efforts to discharge any part of her debt to him, she had at first offered to pay him a part of her passage money out of her generous wages. Michael had met her offer with a raised brow and a blunt refusal.

"My thanks," he had said dryly some days back, when she had cornered him on the staircase. "But I believe I told you earlier—you owe me nothing."

"With such a sum your tailor could make up an

elegant coat, and—and I would be very happy," she had insisted, becoming inarticulate in her earnestness.

"You are suggesting you could be happy with me—simply in a new coat? Oh, Katharine," he mocked. "Have not your Tory leanings taught you yet that you can't make a silk purse out of a sow's ear?"

"You are not a sow's ear," she denied hotly, and then could not help laughing with him. But she had returned obstinately to the point she was trying to make. "If you were well turned out, like Edmund, perhaps the quality——"

"You want me to cater to the carriage trade, not the rabble, is that it?"

"Yes," she confessed.

"Why?"

"Why not?" Katharine countered, looking up at him. "Oh, Michael—" She spread her hands in a pleading gesture. "In a little while you could afford a chaise of your own, a house——"

"And a wife perhaps?"

She had not thought as far as this, and the suggestion, coming from him so coolly, took her aback.

He leaned lazily against the banister and regarded her through eyes amused, yet speculative.

"Whom do you have in mind for my spouse, if I may ask?"

"No one, just yet," she answered truthfully. "First you must——"

"Make myself a dandy," he supplied. "Lace at the

wrists, buckles of genuine silver on my shoes, and a gold-headed cane?"

"Michael," she implored. "I am serious!"

"So am I." He moved down a step, lifted a dark curl from her neck, and then dropped it lightly back into place. "My dear Katharine, in French silk or homespun, silver or pinchbeck, I shall treat those who call on me. Tory or rebel—white or black—" He shrugged. "I care not. Only that I may be of some service."

"You will never have two shillings to your name!" she burst out, angered beyond reason at his stubbornness.

"Don't be too sure. I may marry a rich widow."

Her brows flew up and she stared at him.

Michael laughed. "Remember, my lovely one, two can play at that game."

"*I* am not playing at it!"

His eyes narrowed. "Are you not? My cousin, I notice, now seeks your advice. Did he not beg your preference of materials for his new evening coat?"

"Yes," she admitted reluctantly, "but——"

"But *I* have not," he finished shortly .

She would not make him a gift at all, were she not so deeply in his debt, Katharine thought now, angered anew at his obstinate pride. But the material she rubbed between thumb and forefinger was of excellent quality, and she knew she must have it, though the cost was staggering.

"Surely the price is exorbitant?" she asked in dismay.

"A little high, of course. Everything has gone up."

"Cambric, too?" For the coat must be lined.

The widow nodded. "That, too, I regret to say."

"And braid?" Katharine held up a length of silk braid.

"Braid, too, unfortunately."

How she would like to rifle Edmund Winter's warehouse, the girl thought rebelliously, as she paid for her purchases. Say what they would, the hateful rebels were pushing prices sky-high by their stubborn insistence on not importing from Britain.

There were strangers abroad on the streets today, handsome marines from the *Canseaux* whose admiring glances were a challenge and a compliment. Like a small peahen Annette preened, smoothing her fair hair beneath a charming bonnet of velvet and plumes.

"It is much more comfortable with a King's ship in the harbor, is it not?" she inquired.

"Yes," Katharine agreed.

"Do you fancy a soldier as a husband?" Annette's eyes were on the scarlet uniforms.

"I cannot say that I do. But once, a long time ago, I fancied a lord," Katharine admitted wryly.

"Did he die?"

"No." Candidly she met the frank gaze turned on her. "He deserted me."

Annette gave a little gasp, and then her hold on her governess's arm tightened. "I shall never desert you," she whispered fiercely. "And you can stay with us forever!"

"Thank you, my darling."

When they arrived in King Street a few minutes later, they found the household in a flurry of activity.

"We shall dine later than usual, for Edmund has asked three of the officers from the *Canseaux* to join us," Mrs. Winter explained. "And Isabella and Robert Dunmore are bringing their house guest, Pamela Cavendish, with them." With an exploratory forefinger she inspected the hall table critically for dust. Then abruptly she turned to Annette, who had carelessly dropped her bonnet on a chair. "Annette! Take your bonnet upstairs out of the way at once, if you please!" she exclaimed sharply. "And Katharine!" She put an anxious hand on the older girl's arm. "You will oblige me by sitting next to Robert Dunmore at dinner. I am counting on you to entertain him. He is as closemouthed as a clam."

Mrs. Winter's fears had been groundless, Katharine reflected a few hours later, for the dinner was going extremely well. The officers, Captain Stuart of the Royal Marines, Mr. Clyde, a ship's lieutenant, and a downy-faced midshipman called Rogerson, were impeccably groomed, beautifully mannered, and of excellent appetite, especially young Rogerson, whose eyes fastened on the food with such relish that she could well imagine the midshipmen's mess. Robert Dunmore proved easy to entertain, once she discovered that his interests, too, lay largely in culinary achievements.

"I confess I do not see how you manage to serve apple dishes at almost any season," he observed now, tasting a concoction of Polly's made of apples and cream, cinnamon, and sugar.

"Polly dries them very successfully, I'm told," Katharine answered gravely, her lips twitching in amusement at young Rogerson's blissful face as he spooned up the dessert.

All during the meal she had struggled to keep from staring at Pamela Cavendish, who reigned like a queen among her courtiers—Captain Stuart resplendent in scarlet and gold on the one side; Michael, darkly handsome in his suit of black silk, on the other. With her narrow face powdered to a fashionable pallor, her hazel eyes luminous as jewels, and her tawny hair piled high, the young widow was dazzling. The pearls at her neck gleamed in the candlelight, and diamond drops sparkled at her ears. A magnificent emerald flashed on one hand. She had put off the black of full mourning, and tonight wore a heavy taffeta gown of pale gray, lavishly trimmed with jet fringe. Until now, Katharine had felt her own new gown, which she had made of ivory silk and trimmed with cascades of ecru lace at the bodice and sleeves, to be something of a triumph. Annette had declared it "elegant," and Mrs. Winter felt it to be in "quiet good taste." But the widow's toilette quite eclipsed her own. In fact, Katharine observed forlornly, neither her hairdo, a pile of black locks lovingly wound with gold ribbon by Annette, nor the small black patch of court plaster hopefully applied to her cheek, gave her the faintest claim to fashion or sophistication. And certainly she could not pretend to any proficiency in the art of coquetry as practiced by the widow.

Fascinated, she watched as Mrs. Cavendish leaned toward Michael and spoke in a husky tone that was almost a caress.

"La, sir!" Her slender fingers tapped his sleeve ever so slightly, and her green eyes laughed into his. "Do not fancy that I believe a word of your flattery!"

Quickly the girl looked away, feeling herself a witness to a scene not meant to be shared. Meeting Captain Stuart's eyes, she summoned a smile and was grateful for his immediate attention.

"Are you aware, Miss Leslie, that we both bear quite famous names?" he asked lightly, inviting discussion.

"I am aware that yours, sir, is a distinguished one certainly," she answered courteously. "Kings and queens bear witness to it."

He laughed, and lifting his wine glass, regarded her humorously over its rim.

"It is certainly true that in times past some of my ancestors made themselves known—in a number of ways," he conceded with an easy smile. "But more recently it was the Leslie name that gained notoriety."

Katharine felt a prick of fear, but she was compelled in common politeness to respond.

"M-mine, sir?" she stammered.

"Yours." He sipped at the wine and then put down the glass. "Someone by your name escaped from Newgate last summer. She was a governess, too, I believe—in for stealing."

Before her eyes the gold and scarlet of his uniform blurred in iridescent colors, and Katharine blinked as she struggled to focus clearly. In the next instant she saw him plainly, smiling, easy, utterly unconscious of the terror his casual words had raised within her—coming like a blow that first dulls the vision, and then slows the heart to heavy, painful strokes.

"I remember that case." Lieutenant Clyde corroborated the words of his fellow officer. "The girl was—er —rather violent, was she not?" He laughed, and Katharine heard in her mind Goss laughing again in mockery and derision. And she felt sick now, sure that her blanched face and trembling hands betrayed her, feeling a constricting fear at her throat, suffocating in its intensity.

"She got clear away aboard ship," Captain Stuart reminisced. "Or was it to Scotland?"

"Scotland, as I recall." Michael's voice, cool, quiet in assurance, reached out to her, and she dared to look up, catching a gleam of compassion in his eyes before he donned the familiar mask of raillery. "Our Miss Leslie has never been known to steal anything," he said lightly. "Except, of course, gentlemen's hearts."

Amid the general laughter, Katharine felt the conversation eddy around her again like a warm tide, leaving her isolated on an island of safety created by Michael's quick wit. She drew a long breath, and when she had composed herself a little, she tried to smile her thanks to him, but he was immersed in conversation with the widow, his attention seemingly devoted to her, and after one or two futile attempts she gave up. Finally Edmund Winter proposed a last toast to the King, and after it his mother signaled the ladies to retire to the drawing room.

"If you will excuse me, ma'am," Katharine murmured. "I shall make sure that Annette is in bed."

"Yes, but come back at once." The duties of hostess still weighed heavily on Mrs. Winter. "We shall need you when the gentlemen join us."

She found Annette ensconced with her dolls and gratefully sank down on the bed among them.

"Are you upset? You're trembling!" Annette missed nothing. "Did something frighten you?"

"Just—just for a moment."

Her pupil's quick mind veered to another subject. "Did Mr. Rogerson dine well? When you all went into the dining room, he looked hungry to me."

"He was. He ate up Polly's pudding very readily."

With careful fingers Annette wound a bit of blue ribbon round the blond locks of one of her dolls; then she looked up.

"Do you think Michael is—is attracted to Mrs. Cavendish?" she asked slowly.

Cautious of her elaborate coiffure, her governess twisted round to face her. "Why do you ask?"

"He stares at her."

Inwardly Katharine acknowledged this truth. But she did not admit it aloud. "I really have not had time to judge," she said carefully.

Annette looked thoughtful. "I think perhaps she smiles too much for a real lady," she observed.

"Oh, Annette!" With a tremulous laugh Katharine touched her cheek to her pupil's. "What a comfort you are!" Rising, she shook out the folds of her ivory gown. "Now I must go back. I do not want to keep your grandmother waiting."

With a swift hand Annette scooped up a napkin from the table. "There is a gingerbread inside for Mr. Rogerson," she explained. "To eat when he gets back to his ship."

"I am sure he will be very grateful." Katharine took the napkin, then bending down kissed Annette's cheek tenderly. "Good night, my love."

A few minutes later she explained the gift to the young officer. He laughed, but his eyes were wistful.

"I have a sister just about your pupil's age, Miss Leslie," he said.

Seeing him straight and tall and very young in the King's uniform, Katharine sensed his nostalgia. "And you miss her?" she asked softly.

"Sometimes, I confess, ma'am, home seems very far away."

"Perhaps you will come again to call on us."

"I should be honored, ma'am." With a slight bow he left her and moved to join the other gentlemen gathered in a half circle round Mrs. Cavendish, whose eyes, responding to their compliments, lit her face like green flames, Katharine saw with a sigh.

She herself moved toward one of the windows, uncurtained as yet, mirroring the candles to the April evening. There had been other dinners, she reflected, and despite her tenuous position she had enjoyed them, finding the gentlemen easy and unconstrained, the ladies cordial. Tonight, in her new gown and careful coiffure, she longed to sparkle, to be confident and assured with the officers, even a little flirtatious, perhaps, with Edmund and Michael. But confronted with such a dazzling competitor she was at a loss, feeling only a helpless fury at herself for caring so much. The officers, of course, would be attracted to the young widow as moths to a candle. And Edmund, as host, must be attentive. But Michael's devotion piqued her more than she cared to admit.

Pretending an indifference to the room and its occupants, she moved closer to one of the windows and stood quietly gazing at the fire opposite. And in that moment there came a splintering of glass, like icicles falling behind her. Katharine leaped aside in fright, feeling as she did so a prick, slight as the touch of a needle, on her shoulder.

"Come away from that window, Katharine!" Above someone's hysterical scream, Michael's voice cut sharply across the room, and then his hand was hard on her arm, thrusting her aside as he snapped the heavy draperies across the window.

"Are you hurt?" he demanded.

"No," she answered quickly. Looking down, she saw in shocked disbelief a rock the size of a man's fist lying on the floor at her feet.

"Michael, will you take charge here while we search outside?"

She looked up to see Edmund and two of the officers. Her employer fixed anxious eyes on her.

"Katharine, have they harmed you?"

"No, sir," she said reassuringly.

Across the room, Isabella Dunmore, with Mrs. Winter at her side, sniffed long draughts of her smelling salts, while Pamela Cavendish, waving a fan of black lace with a languid hand, lay back against the sofa, attended by Robert Dunmore and young Rogerson. Rome appeared now with a decanter and glasses, offering wine as a restorative.

Michael's voice touched Katharine's ear. "Come into the kitchen with me. There is blood on the neck of your gown."

Polly supplied a basin of hot water, and Michael washed his hands quickly. Then, while the old servant held a candle close, he carefully drew out a long sliver of glass that had pierced the lace of Katharine's gown and cut into her shoulder. Wiping the wound with hot water, he pressed a clean napkin lightly against it.

"The bleeding should stop in a moment." With sharp

eyes he scanned her face and neck. "Thank God there seems to be no other damage. You will oblige me by staying quiet a few minutes."

She was glad to obey, for suddenly a heavy, dragging fatigue overwhelmed her. Trying to relax, she closed her eyes, only to see immediately Captain Stuart's bland and smiling face and to hear his words again echoing in her mind. She shuddered at the memory.

"What is it?" Michael asked quickly.

"I—I was recalling dinner." She looked up into his face. "Oh, Michael, I am deeply grateful to you for speaking when you did."

"Never mind your gratitude. Have you told my cousin yet of your sojourn in Newgate?"

"No," she whispered.

"If you are to realize your hopes in that quarter, I think you had best inform him," he said dryly. "Better you than another."

Lifting the napkin, he waited a moment, his eyes on the cut. "You can go up now, I think. If it should begin to bleed again, you have only to call me. I shall make your excuses to the company."

"But——"

"You are exhausted, that is quite obvious," he said shortly. "Besides, the party is over. Neither Edmund nor the whole British fleet will find the rebels who tossed that rock through the window." He scanned her face. "Don't look so woebegone, I beseech you," he said with a little laugh. "In ten minutes the officers will return to their ship, and I must see the charming Pamela safely to her door."

"Of course." For some reason the weariness deepened. "She is very beautiful," Katharine conceded, "like —like a queen."

"Exactly," he agreed. "A regal figure, imperial manners, and six thousand pounds a year. She can command any man."

Picking up a candle, he lighted her over the back stairs. The evening had been a singular failure, she thought wretchedly as she followed him. And to be marched to bed like a small child seemed the crowning indignity.

Touching the wall sconce into flame, Michael turned to gaze down at her, his eyes gleaming darkly.

"How come you to be wearing a patch?" he demanded. "Is not this a new acquisition?"

Her hand flew to her face, touching the small round of court plaster she had placed with such hopes at the corner of her mouth.

"It—it is the mode," she stammered defensively. "And I hoped it would make me l-look older."

"Oh, it does," he agreed blandly. "In fact you look to be quite a woman of the world."

Suspicious of his tone, she glanced up.

He laughed, and taking a quick step toward her, placed his fingers beneath her chin. Tipping her head back, he looked full into her eyes, his own black with intent.

"But you should take care where you place one, should you not, ma'am? A patch in such a place invites only one response."

Bending his head he kissed her, swiftly but with emphasis, upon the mouth.

14

The hurling of a rock through Edmund Winter's window was more than an act of casual vandalism, Katharine realized as the spring days wore on. The defiant deed was a symbol of the deepening hatred toward the King's men and the King's friends. On the twenty-first of April news of a battle between British soldiers and Massachusetts farmers at Lexington swept the town, and within forty-eight hours a company of soldiers had set out from Falmouth to aid the rebel cause. Meanwhile, members of a town meeting hastily resolved to borrow money for more powder and guns.

"It is civil war now," Edmund Winter groaned.

In the house on King Street the curtains were drawn tight; the doors were bolted. The stablemen took turns keeping watch of the horses. Tory and rebel alike had already lost fine mounts to the marching militia.

In the harbor rode His Majesty's Ship *Canseaux*, but although her commander was constantly urged by Captain Coulson and other prominent Tories to check the rebels' actions, Captain Mowat made no move. When two small tenders of His Majesty's fleet arrived in the bay, the Tories took heart. Combined with the *Canseaux*, here, surely, were the means to subdue the rebel element! They watched in cold satisfaction as families, fearful of immediate bombardment, bundled their belongings into carts and wagons and sent them out of town. But the satisfaction was short-lived. The tenders made their way to Boston and offered no help.

Walking on Munjoy's Hill one May afternoon in search of the pink and fragrant blossoms of the trailing arbutus, Katharine and Annette were astonished to be stopped by a man with a sprig of spruce in his hat and a musket in his hand.

"Can't go no farther, ma'am." Politely he touched his hat to Katharine. "I'll ask you to turn back now, if you please."

"But why?" Annette exclaimed.

"Might not be safe for two ladies to come any farther along the path just now." Meeting Katharine's, his eyes were resolute.

"Come along, Annette." She took her pupil's hand. "We can try the wood behind the orchard."

The wood yielded abundant Mayflowers, and the

evening brought an explanation of the sentinel on the hill.

"The rebels under Colonel Thompson, a hothead from Brunswick, seized Captain Mowat, his ship's surgeon, and the Anglican minister, John Wiswall, as they were walking on Munjoy's Hill this afternoon," Edmund announced on his return from his warehouse. The veins of his face had darkened, and his voice was hoarse with anger. "Thompson could not be prevailed upon to release his prisoners until it was pointed out that the town is almost without flour and corn. The ship bringing a supply is due any day now. The fool! What chance does he think a small vessel would have of getting into port if a King's armed ship chose to block the way? The town could starve! Not until General Preble and Colonel Freeman, both responsible men, thank God, had pledged themselves as hostages, would Thompson agree to release his prisoners. All three men —Captain Mowat, the ship's surgeon, and Wiswall— are at liberty now, but they have given their parole to deliver themselves up for a reckoning with the rebels tomorrow." He sank into a chair and with a trembling hand took the glass of wine Rome offered. "Good God! Seizing the captain of a King's ship! What can Thompson be thinking of? If the *Canseaux* blows the town to bits, it will be just punishment for such an outrage!"

"You forget," Michael interposed. His face was grave and his tone was tempered to a quiet firmness. "Since the bloodshed at Lexington and Concord, many of the rebels consider themselves at war with England. Colonel Thompson may well regard the men he has seized as prisoners of war."

By the next morning militia from Gorham, Scarborough, Cape Elizabeth, and Stroudwater had marched into Falmouth, determined to destroy the *Canseaux*. But no one could agree on how to proceed against a man-of-war with guns leveled directly into the town. Moreover, though the militia might regard the destruction of the ship as imperative, many of the townspeople did not. When, however, it appeared that Captain Mowat did not intend to honor his parole and come on shore to face the rebels, the militia demanded that General Preble and Colonel Freeman, whom they had confined all day as hostages for the missing captain, furnish refreshment for the military men then in the town. The number was staggering—well over three hundred. Bread, cheese, and two barrels of rum for each company were supplied.

"Half of the men are drunk now," Edmund said bitterly, as he examined the latched shutters of the windows. All of the family, except Annette, who had retired, were gathered in the drawing room. "By midnight they will be completely out of control and the town will be in a pretty state!"

Katharine drew nearer the fire, recalling with a shudder the revels and riots of Newgate when the extortion money from a new prisoner bought gin and wine.

A sudden pounding of the door knocker brought Michael to his feet, and he sent his cousin a long look.

"Rome, open the door!" his master shouted.

The two men who were ushered into the room a moment later looked sober enough, Katharine saw in relief, as she and Mrs. Winter acknowledged their bows with brief nods.

Edmund wasted no words. "Well, Enoch, how can I serve you?" he asked, addressing the older of the men.

"We are requested by the Board of War now in charge of the town government to summon you, Edmund Winter, to the Town House," the man replied formally.

"For what reason?"

"To answer charges of being a Tory."

Edmund drew himself up. "If to be a Tory is to be loyal to His Majesty's Government, then I am one." He turned to his cousin. "Michael, will you see to things here?"

"Unless you want me to go with you."

"No, thank you. I shall go alone."

When Edmund was gone, the room fell into a taut stillness that slackened only when a log on the fire crackled. In the candlelight Mrs. Winter's face was gray, her lips drawn tight, and to Katharine she seemed suddenly to have become a very old woman. The girl seethed with renewed outrage. How dare the rebel leaders inflict such terrible anxiety! Longing to be of comfort, she said quietly, "Let me get you a cup of tea, ma'am, or a little wine."

"Thank you, Katharine. But I believe if Michael will give me his arm, I shall go to my room. Then, if I want anything, Polly can bring it to me."

Michael lighted her up the stairs and was quickly back.

"This sort of thing could kill her!" Katharine stormed, her skirts sweeping the hearth as she paced to and fro. "How dare they commit such an outrage!"

Michael came to stand beside her. "The town is now under military law," he said quietly. "The officers will accord Edmund every respect, I am sure. But some of the men are already out of hand. Do you hear that noise?"

From the street now there came songs, hoarse shouts, catcalls, and finally, a shattering of glass.

"Michael!" She looked at him in shock. "That's close!"

"Yes, Captain Coulson's house, I fear."

"You mean they are—they are *breaking in?*"

"I mean just that," he answered grimly. "I hope to God the family is safe."

"What about us?"

He shrugged. "When men are drunk and ill disciplined, anything can happen." Then, seeing her blanched face and frightened eyes, he caught up her hands. "Don't tremble so! I doubt very much if they come here, and if they do—" His voice was dry and there was a flicker of jest in it. "Your lack of faith in me as a champion is not very flattering, is it?"

She laughed a little, but the moment of lightness passed swiftly as the splintering of glass came again and the voices on the street grew more raucous.

Her thoughts veered to Edmund. "If those men see Edmund on his way to the Town House—" she whispered. In Maine and Massachusetts there had been Tories cruelly tarred and feathered, she knew, feeling suddenly sick with apprehension.

"I should have insisted on going with him." Michael strode toward the hall. "Do you need Rome? He's with the boys in the stable."

"No, oh, no!" She hastened after him. "I'll keep everything locked. Oh, do hurry!" she begged, as he unbolted the door.

"I'll give four knocks when we return—at this door," he instructed, and slipped out.

She snapped the bolt into place and went back to the fire, but she could not stay still. Restlessly she circled the room, checking the shutters. Then, moving on, she examined the dining room, the flicker of her candle casting long shadows on the walls, bringing into dull glimmer the silver candelabra on the sideboard, and somehow intensifying the black cloth shrouding the cage of the parakeet. Should she go up to Mrs. Winter? No, it was not really necessary. Polly was there, and the old slave was beloved by her mistress.

She returned to the drawing room. There was noth-

ing to do but wait, and she sat down on the velvet hassock, feeling as nervous as the cat who appeared now
to pace round her skirts, unhappily aware of some secret
threat. Katharine looked out over the room, familiar and
charming with its graceful furnishings in rosewood and
brocade. The odor of the beeswax with which Polly
polished so diligently, combined with the hot smell of
candle grease from the wall sconces, was a part of the
intimacy, the happy nostalgia she had shared here with
the family. And tonight the fragrance of the Mayflowers,
intensified by the warmth from the fire, gave an unbe-
lievable sweetness to the air. How she had come to love
this room—as if it were her own.

She moved into the kitchen and made herself a cup
of tea. Polly's kitchen always gleamed, reflecting the old
woman's devotion as a scrubbed child reflects a doting
mother, Katharine thought with a smile. Sanded and
brushed, the floor was smooth and white with care.
Above the hearth the copper pots and kettles shone
bright as suns. Sitting in front of the fire, she sipped
her tea. From the street the noise was less now, except
for a strange murmur she could not identify. She had
not checked the kitchen, she realized, and going to the
window she saw that here there was no shutter, and the
window itself was slightly open. And now she recognized
the sound she heard—voices. Just below the window
two men were arguing in hoarse whispers. Hastily Katharine drew against the wall, suddenly paralyzed with
terror.

"Edmund Winter's house, ain't it?" One voice was loud and ugly.

"Aye, but you'll not smash the windows of friends, Eben." The response was firm.

"Friends! Winter is a Tory, ain't he? Big, fat, merchant Tory?"

"Maybe. But his cousin ain't."

"Who's his cousin?"

"Michael Edes."

"Is he one of us?" The rough voice was belligerent.

"He's not one of them."

"What do I owe the likes o' him?"

"You'd best answer that yourself, Eben. I owe him the twins and Prue's good health."

The man spat. "Ye're soft, John Bates, soft as a woman."

"Maybe. Come along. There's good wine in Coulson's cellars, and our friends are drinking it all up."

The men stumbled off in the darkness, and Katharine drew a deep breath. Their immunity this night they owed to Michael, she thought with a grateful heart— Michael, who made no distinction between Tory and rebel in their need of him.

Returning to the drawing room, she stirred up the fire. But she could not stay still. Whistles and shouts still rang in the street, and the occasional crack of a bottle shattered the night. As the minutes crawled by, her anxiety deepened. Surely now they should be back? She paced before the hearth, stole to the windows to peer through the shutters, lingered in the hall. When at last four knocks, steady and firm, sounded, she snatched up her candle, almost extinguishing its small flame in her eagerness to reach the door. But her whisper was cautious.

"Michael?"

"Yes. Open up."

She drew back the bolt and the two men entered.

Edmund looked as urbane and elegant as always, and Michael, taking the candle from her unsteady hand, moved with the same easy grace. Relief at seeing them both unharmed washed over her in a flood of thankfulness, sweeping aside all formalities, and her voice broke as she stammered, "Oh, th-thank God!"

"Katharine! What is it?" her employer exclaimed anxiously.

Embarrassed by her own emotion, and acutely aware of Michael's keen eyes upon her, she quickly composed herself.

"It is nothing, sir," she murmured. "It is just that you are safe."

"My dear girl, we are safe and sound, as you can see." He gathered up her hands in his and kissed them, and she saw with dismay that her impulsive greeting had meant far more than she had intended. For a long moment Edmund looked into her face, and she felt her cheeks burn under his fervent glance. Then he released her hands and turned toward the stairs. "You will excuse me. I must let my mother know that all is well."

"Come along." Michael's hand was beneath her elbow. "You sound as though you could do with some nourishment."

"I've had tea."

"I had in mind something a little stronger."

She sat on the sofa and let him bring her mulled wine, the antidote for every weakness. But she did not really need a comforting draught. Now, with the household restored to normalcy and the sounds in the street diminished, she felt as if a siege had been lifted, and the castle and its occupants were once again secure.

Michael thrust the footstool beneath her feet and sank down in a chair close to the fire.

"Edmund acquitted himself well," he said, sipping his wine. "But he left no doubt as to his position. He refused to deny his admiration for Thomas Hutchinson, the former royal governor whose personal letters fell into the hands of the rebels and have been used to discredit him. Edmund signed a complimentary address to the governor some time back, and despite all pressure, he stands by his signature."

"Why should he deny it?"

"Some men feel that Hutchinson, when he was governor, tried to subvert the charter rights. Unfortunately, in one of his letters he does speak of the necessity for lessening English liberties here in the colonies."

"But I thought Governor Hutchinson had gone to England!"

"He did, months ago."

Katharine frowned. "Then the rebels are using this as——"

"As one means of determining where a man stands."

"It's outrageous!"

"Edmund has the courage of his convictions," he said gravely. "I admire him for his honesty. He admits that he has not observed the fast days set by the Continental Congress—nor does he intend to." Putting down his glass, he turned to her more fully, a derisive note creeping into his voice. "You will be interested to learn that our friend Robert Dunmore has published in the *Essex Gazette* his heartfelt repentance at signing the address to Hutchinson. His remorse even extends to the dinner party honoring the King's officers—given here, you may recall. Dunmore declares himself now in full sympathy with the present government."

Katharine's eyes blazed. "The wretched turncoat!"

"Many men are doing the same. He has a lot at stake —a wife, children, property—even the beautiful Widow Cavendish on his hands," he finished laconically.

"Oh, Michael!" she cried in anguish. "Where will it end?"

"God knows. Edmund is admired for his courage, hated for his convictions." She saw his glance go to the door. "Yes, Polly?"

"There's a man wants to see you, sir—quick, he says," Polly answered.

As Michael pulled himself from his chair, Katharine heard his indrawn sigh and could see his weariness. She longed to aid in some way, but there was nothing she could do, she realized helplessly. Gathering up her skirts, she rose, too, and drew a little closer to the comfort of the fire.

Michael was quickly back. "I must bid you good night," he said with a wry smile. "Some fool in Mrs. Greele's tavern shot off his musket a few minutes ago and wounded one of his comrades in arms."

"Michael!" She touched his sleeve anxiously. "For heaven's sake, take care!"

He drew up, his own hand covering hers. "I am flattered by your anxiety on my behalf, dear lady," he said in suave tones. "I had thought your concern must have already been exhausted on my cousin."

Looking up, she caught the glint of mockery in his eyes, and snatched away her hand.

"It is true," she said slowly. "I do feel a deep concern for Edmund." She raised her lashes and met his gaze blandly, determined to pay him back. "But for you, sir, I have always a *little* regard."

He laughed, lifted her hand and brushed it with his lips, and went out into the night.

For several days Falmouth existed under the control of the unruly militia. At last, wearied by their exertions, the soldiers went back to their homes. Almost immediately Captain Mowat in the *Canseaux* and Captain Coulson in his new mast ship weighed anchor. Once again the town breathed freely.

Katharine was now seriously concerned about the family's future. Although Mrs. Winter could be imperious in her demands, she held her in warm affection. Edmund she had come to respect deeply for his integrity and courage. Annette she loved. What was to become of them—and of her? Already one or two Tory families had sought refuge in New York, a Loyalist stronghold. Certainly here in Falmouth there was no longer any place for Edmund Winter. The aristocratic merchant was being slowly frozen out. The icy stares he encountered on the street could be ignored, but the embargo on his goods—cheeses from Holland, silks from France, even domestic flour, a commodity usually in great demand—had a more telling effect. It was becoming impossible for him to find buyers for his incoming cargoes, even though they were not of British manufacture. It was becoming equally difficult to procure the lumber and dried fish he had for years exported. Some merchants bluntly refused to do business with him. Others were afraid to be seen in his company, lest they, too, be branded with the hateful name of "Tory."

Indeed, the uncertainty had its effect on everyone, the girl thought unhappily, as she and Annette sat this late May day on a rustic bench beneath the apple blossoms of the orchard. Never a strong student, Annette was becoming demoralized under the shifting family fortunes, and Katharine was hard put to keep her pupil's attention on her lessons. But although she found it difficult to bring Annette's mind to bear long on anything

academic, she could guide her young fingers in the practical fashioning of a waistcoat, made of contraband
brocade smuggled from the warehouse on Fore Street.

"I do wish I could bind a buttonhole as you do."
Annette sighed as she watched her governess's nimble
fingers on the silk.

"You will very soon. See how straight your seams are
now, and recall what they once were!" With a smile
Katharine handed back the waistcoat. "Now you try,"
she encouraged, picking up the serge coat she herself
was working on, and wondering if she would ever have
the courage to present it to Michael.

"It's true, I am better than I was," Annette agreed,
happily plying her needle. "And Father will be very
surprised to find that a piece of cloth he gave *me* has
been made into a gift for *him!*" She looked up. "Oh,
Katharine, here he comes now! You must hide this
under Michael's coat or he will see it!" She thrust the
silk under the serge and ran to greet her parent. For a
minute they talked together; then Annette hastened
toward the house.

Katharine put down her work and looked up to smile
a welcome. "You are earlier than usual today, sir."

"Yes." He sank down heavily beside her, and she saw
in the afternoon sunlight how the lines of his face had
deepened. But there was no other sign of distress. Pride
of person and of place kept Edmund Winter meticu-
lously groomed, his suit rich and elegant as always, his
carriage and demeanor that of an English gentleman.

"Katharine, I must speak with you," he said quietly.

Instantly she knew that some momentous decision had been reached; feared, too, with a shiver of dread, that her own confession could be delayed no longer.

"It is evident that we cannot remain longer here in Falmouth, though it has been our home for nearly twenty years." In a helpless gesture he spread his hands to the orchard and the woods beyond. "I can neither sell nor buy. The *Claire* is due any day now from Holland, but she will have to go on to New York to unload, I fear." He looked down at her with a faint smile, and when he spoke again his voice was more cheerful. "However, in some ways I am fortunate. There is the farm in England to return to, self-sufficient, and with a charming house on the property, besides the tenants' dwellings. I am not destitute, thank heaven." He turned to her, and now she knew that the declaration she had dreamed of was coming; but she felt no triumph as she had expected, only a desperate urgency to forestall his words, halt the commitment he was about to make, until she herself had spoken.

"Please, sir——"

He interrupted, taking her hand. "Will you come back to England as governess?" he asked eagerly. "Then, when we are settled there, I should be honored if you——"

"*Please, sir.*" Gently she withdrew her hand and put firm fingers on his arm. "I beg that you will hear me out."

Slowly she told him of Lady Blaize, of Jay, of Michael, of Newgate. And as she spoke, her voice—low, thin, hurrying forward—echoed in her ears like the voice in a dream. She felt her palms grow wet as she recalled the nightmare days and nights of prison, and her voice trembled as she spoke of Mary and Billy. But almost as soon as she mentioned Newgate, she sensed Edmund's antipathy, and finally glancing up into his face, she saw it cold and withdrawn, implacable in its sternness, and knew it was useless to go on. She stopped, and the quiet of the May afternoon descended on them. When he still did not speak, she said hesitantly, "You see, sir, why I can never return to England. It would mean risking imprisonment again."

"Nor can I continue to harbor a fugitive from the King's justice," he said heavily, with a chill dignity she had never heard. "But that is apparently what I have done—what I am doing, in fact."

"But I am innocent!" Katharine cried.

"Innocent or guilty, it makes no difference." His voice was stony in its coldness. "I know the law. Michael knows the law. In aiding you to escape he chose deliberately to break it."

For an instant she was speechless, then anger swirled up in a red mist before her eyes, blinding in its intensity. "*Fourteen years!*" she cried passionately. "Have you thought of that—in days, in weeks, in months? I would have died had I been forced to stay there!"

"That is beside the point," he said remorselessly.

"One of you—Michael, certainly—should have informed me of your sentence."

Katharine drew herself up. "Michael is not to blame," she said quietly. "He told me to be honest with you. It is I who am at fault."

Edmund came to his feet and stared down at her. When he spoke, his words were precise, but painfully labored. "I hold you in deep affection, Katharine," he said slowly. "But I have also my principles." Above the lace at his throat his face looked ravaged, and she saw now that in saving herself from his censure these many weeks, she had allowed ample time for his affection to ripen. That it had was evident now as he struggled between his duty, as he saw it, and his regard for her. She had foreseen no such conflict as this, and knowing she had deliberately sought his devotion, she was stricken with remorse, longing to alleviate his hurt and to beg his forgiveness. She reached out to him, but he drew back sharply, and her hand fluttered down to her side.

"Why did you not tell me?" he demanded in baffled tones.

Now, too late, she met his question honestly. "I was afraid," she whispered, looking into her own heart with ruthless candor, while the words she sought came slowly, pitiless in their truth. "And I wanted—after Newgate—I wanted at all costs the security of a home."

He bowed stiffly, turned on his heel, and left her.

Under the apple blossoms she sat alone, suffused by a deepening shame as she measured the full depth of her deceit. She had entered his house a stranger, hidden the one blemish she feared would condemn her in his eyes, and become a cherished member of the family. And while she had taught Annette to the best of her ability, she had not scrupled to use her position to entrench herself. Had she lost her heart to Edmund, had she nourished a growing affection for him as he had for her, there might be some excuse. But her heart had never been touched. Nor could she deny knowing full well what his reaction to her confession might be. From the day of her arrival she had seen his abhorrence of lawlessness, his antipathy to the rebels, his insistence on loyalty and obedience to the King's laws. No matter that on her those laws had inflicted a terrible wrong and hardship. Edmund honored them and the men who executed them—judge, Parliament, and King.

Edmund, she saw now, was like the rock along the coast that held back the sea. Hard, rooted, he stood by his beliefs with the steadfastness of a cliff, wearing a little under the strain of the tides, but refusing to crumble. Like a barnacle clinging to a rock, she had tried to attach herself to his strength. But she had been pulled away by a contrary tide, and now, dislodged, uncertain, rolling loose in the shifting sands of this new world, she found herself alone—caught up in a rip current of opposing forces, Tory and rebel.

15 {

A resolve of the Provincial Congress forbidding Tories to carry their effects out of the country prevented Edmund Winter from loading his household goods aboard the *Claire* when she arrived in Falmouth. The house and its furnishings, the warehouse and its contents, were, in fact, no longer his to dispose of. After heated debate the Committee of Safety allowed him his ship and his cargo, granting him a permit to sail for London within ten days.

"A gracious gesture, certainly," he remarked in bitter tones this June morning. "I am permitted to sail in my own ship, carry my own cargo, in the company of my own family!"

Katharine saw the sardonic twist of his mouth as he

turned to his cousin. "What if I deed the house and warehouse to you, Michael?"

Michael shook his head. "It's a scheme that wouldn't work. Possibly all of your possessions will be sold eventually to support the rebel cause. And although I thank you for your generous thought, I have need of neither house nor warehouse. Yesterday I made the first payment on my purchase of the old Wilson place in Back Street."

"Back Street!" his cousin exclaimed.

"Not the most fashionable quarter, I grant you. But it has its advantages."

"Well, I am thankful to learn that the days and nights you have given to your patients have brought you some reward at last," Mrs. Winter said in somewhat tart tones. "Your devotion to that poor Smith family this past week must have been exceptionally wearing. But why, pray, did you choose Back Street? It is so far from the center of things."

"Not really, ma'am." Michael smiled. "It is convenient to the country as well as to town. And I chose this particular house because it is small and cozy, and there is a room at the back I can use as a surgery. And," he added significantly, "the price is within my means."

"But is it furnished, Michael?" his aunt inquired dubiously.

"There are beds, ma'am, some pots and pans, a table, one or two chairs—" He broke off. "And the Widow Nolan will see to my wants."

Mrs. Winter raised her brows. "Is she still about?"

"Hale and hearty at seventy-three."

His cousin gave a little chuckle. "What about the Widow Cavendish?" he challenged.

Katharine drew a quick breath and bent her head more closely to the lace frill she was mending for Mrs. Winter. Several times after the family had attended services at St. Paul's, Michael had accompanied the young widow home. Though she would have found it hard to give convincing reasons for her feelings, she did not want Michael to wed the handsome widow.

In answer to his cousin's question, Michael gave a wry laugh. "Alas, my house, I fear, would scarcely be to her taste."

His aunt sent him a shrewd look. "Pamela Cavendish has a large fortune and friends now in the right places. She could be of immense help to you in your practice here."

Her nephew nodded. "I know, and it grieves me deeply that I cannot take advantage of this fact." He spread his hands in a gesture of mock despair. "But you would not have me offer for her, would you, dear madam, if my heart were not in it?"

Catching his grin, Mrs. Winter laughed in spite of herself. "You are incorrigible!" she exclaimed. Then her eyes brightened. "But why shouldn't the family silver go to you? To be sure, Edmund has given his word that nothing shall accompany us out of the country. Well, it need not!" Another gleam lighted her face. "What about china and linen?"

"I have not had time to give them much thought, ma'am, and I beg that you will do nothing that might bring on censure from the Committee."

As the conversation fell to family heirlooms, Katharine mused on her own plans. Since their unhappy talk in the orchard, her employer had treated her a little more formally but no less kindly, while his mother, regretting that Katharine must endure the uncertainties of life in a land now ruled by republicans and levelers, had written an old friend in New York recommending the girl highly as a governess. Newgate had never once been mentioned, and Katharine was grateful for the delicate manners that made these last days as pleasant for her as possible.

No such polite restraints had curbed Annette's warm affections, however. At Katharine's announcement that she would not accompany them to England, she had flung herself into her teacher's arms in a storm of tears.

"Someday you will come back to Falmouth, my darling." Katharine held the wet cheek close to her own. "Who can tell? Perhaps by next spring you will be sleeping in this very chamber!"

"But—but you will be in someone else's family!" Annette's anguished words cut through her sobs.

"If I am, I shall demand a holiday at once in order to visit you," Katharine comforted. "Believe me, you will always have a place in my heart."

Yet finding a new position was not easy, she discovered. An advertisement in the *Essex Gazette*, stating her qualifications as a governess, had yielded no response, and she had begun to grow anxious. What if no one wanted her? There was no longer any place for her here. The house would be closed, not even the slaves remaining. Polly would go to England as servant to her mistress. Rome and Sam would seek new places, for, fulfilling an old promise, Edmund Winter had granted the slaves their freedom.

"I had not thought they would be so overjoyed," Mrs. Winter had confided in aggrieved tones to Katharine. "It is not as if Edmund were not a good master—there is none better!"

"But to be free, ma'am!" To Katharine the slaves' joyous response was easy to understand. "To be at liberty——"

"Liberty! The word is on every tongue!"

Katharine was silenced. Who could explain to Mrs. Winter the ecstasy of freedom? The simple joy of choosing—be it morning gown or master? To be a slave was to be a prisoner, no matter how warm the shelter, how kind the lord. To be free, she thought with the poignancy of one who has been incarcerated, is to walk in the sun in dignity and gladness.

She came back to the present to hear Mrs. Winter ending a discussion of family china. Now Edmund rose and turned with a bow to his mother and Katharine.

"If you will excuse me, I have work that cannot wait."

"And I shall return to my chamber." His mother stood and shook out her skirts. "I want to look over my gowns in the morning light before I decide which I shall take with me and which I shall bequeath to my friends." Taking her son's arm she moved with him out into the hall.

Michael turned to Katharine. "Can you spare a moment?"

"Certainly."

"I do not know your plans, but I have, I hope, persuaded Edmund to sail, weather and wind permitting, the day after tomorrow. A British warship, the *Senegal*, and two tenders arrived in the harbor this morning. It would be wise for him to leave, I think, while these ships offer protection."

"So soon!" she exclaimed in dismay.

"The sooner the better," he said grimly. "Though neither Edmund nor my aunt will admit it, they must certainly realize how fortunate they will be to escape with a ship and a cargo at their disposal!"

Katharine turned to him, her blue eyes dark with distress. "Oh, Michael," she exclaimed, "what am I to do?"

"You've had no answer to your advertisement?"

"None."

The frown on his forehead deepened, and she saw as she looked at him more closely how drawn his features were beneath the tan of wind and sun. Mrs. Winter had referred to one of his patients, a member of the Smith family who had been desperately ill. Michael had been gone from home almost constantly this past week. But what results this faithful vigil had borne, Katharine had not inquired. She was ashamed now to have taken so little interest, and to add her burdens to those he already carried.

"My aunt had hoped to find a place for you with one of her friends," he said slowly. "Now, I fear, there will not be time." Moving to the mantel, he leaned against it, and there was weariness in every line of his body. Looking down at her, he spoke again. "I can offer you shelter in my house, of course, though even with the Widow Nolan there, people would probably gossip." For a moment he was silent, then a faint smile touched his lips and he spoke more deliberately. "Of course, if worse comes to worst, if you are in truly desperate straits—you could marry me."

Katharine flung the frill aside and leapt to her feet. "Don't be absurd!" she cried impatiently. "Can't you be serious?"

"How do you know that I am not?" The question snapped back at her like a whip, cutting her assurance to shreds and leaving her stunned. She had no time to recover, for his next sentence followed fast, though his words were leisurely and unhurried, delivered in the familiar, mocking tone she knew so well. "But you are right," he agreed, his dark eyes derisive as they met hers. "Had I been really serious, I should have purchased a more pretentious dwelling, should I not?"

Stung to the quick, she winced under this thrust.

Struggling to summon a reply past the sudden tears that welled in her throat, she stumbled into speech. "Perhaps I am not so mercenary as you think me," she stammered painfully.

His cool glance moved over her in a long, full look, and she stiffened under it, determined not to let him see the depth of her hurt. When he spoke again, his words came curt and harsh, flung down in a challenge.

"Could you be mother, nurse, teacher, *and* servant to three children bereft of both parents?" he demanded.

"I could try."

He measured her mercilessly. "Tomorrow?"

"Yes."

"I should warn you, Katharine." Stepping away from the wall, he came to stand before her—tall and straight and hard. "This will not be a comfortable home. There will be no luxuries—and no wages. These are poor people."

How he must despise her to think her as grasping as this!

She raised her head. "I am willing to try," she replied steadily, accepting the challenge.

"Very well. Be ready by ten in the morning." Again his eyes studied her in deliberate appraisal, and the look was a little less condemning, she saw in relief, as he turned aside and left her.

Late that afternoon she was summoned to Mrs. Winter's chamber. The canopied bed was piled high with gowns, ribbons, laces, bonnets, and shawls. Ignoring all these, the older woman turned to her with a smile, flourishing a letter in her hand.

"This message came in on Stephen Waite's ship this afternoon from New York," she said happily. "Stephen himself delivered it to me. Despite his rebel leanings, he is still a gentleman, I am thankful to say." She drew Katharine to the bedside. "My friend Theresa Pettingill wants you to come at once to New York to work in the family of her nephew. This is a splendid opportunity, Katharine." Her voice held her satisfaction. "The Pettingills are an old and established family of fine reputation and considerable wealth. It will be just the place for you."

Katharine's heart leaped. Then she recalled her promise to Michael.

"I—I should like nothing better, ma'am," she stammered. "But unfortunately I have given my promise to Michael to help in the Smith household."

Mrs. Winter stared at her. "You mean he has suggested that you care for those three children in a house where there is not even a kitchenmaid?" she asked incredulously.

"I offered, ma'am."

"Michael must be lost to all reason," his aunt said impatiently. Then her face cleared. "But, of course, now that this opportunity has presented itself, he will release you from your promise. You have only to ask."

All too easily Katharine could imagine Michael's dark eyes gleaming in contempt as she made this request, his smile mocking her as he granted it. No, she thought, stung by pride and a grim resolution to prove herself— no, she would never ask it of him.

"Michael will help you make all the arrangements necessary, I am sure," Mrs. Winter continued, and it was evident that in her mind the matter was closed. "Edmund is too concerned with his own affairs to be asked to do anything more just now."

Giving Katharine the letter, she turned to the bed and selected two of the topmost gowns, one in dove-gray silk, the other of heavy, black serge.

"These are not very dashing," she said, bestowing them on the girl. "But the material is good. You can easily cut them down and make them over to fit you. And I very much hope you will make use of them." Then her voice hardened to a tone Katharine had never heard, and the words came harsh and stinging in their bitterness. "It will give me the greatest pleasure to know that if the gowns are on your back, there will be two less encompassing some dirty rebel neck!"

16

It was a forlorn group that greeted her the next day, Katharine saw in pity, as she surveyed the grave-eyed children standing before her. Their father, Jacob Smith, was gone, killed during the winter months bringing masts out of the forests for the King's ships; and Rebecca, his wife, had died only a few days back, giving birth to a premature child who lay with her now in the graveyard on Munjoy's Hill. These harsh facts Michael had related, and from his taut, bitter tone Katharine had sensed the young doctor's feelings of inadequacy and wretchedness that neither his medical knowledge nor techniques had been enough to save the mother and child.

Ben, a tousle-haired boy of thirteen, stepped forward

now with a brief bow, while the girl, Rachel, clutching the hand of her smaller brother, Jonathan, a rosy child of fifteen months, went down in a curtsy. The quick dip threw the baby off balance, and collapsing in a rumple of petticoats, he set up a wail. With a laugh Michael gathered him up, while Katharine secured Rachel's hand in her own warm clasp.

"You are a very fine housekeeper," she said gently, aware of the strict neatness of the tiny parlor, and longing to erase somehow a little of the grief in the small, tense face upturned to hers.

"Thank you, ma'am."

"I do not know how much help I can be to you," Katharine admitted honestly, feeling keenly her own shortcomings before this quiet child of eleven with her sober brown eyes. "But I shall try."

These words beat repeatedly in her mind the following weeks as she struggled with the countless chores of the household. From morning till night she labored, and still the work was never done. How much she had always taken for granted! In every house she had ever known there had always been someone else to wash, press, preserve, scour, and scrub.

As she and Rachel thrust the family wash into a tub of rain water, heated laboriously this July morning, she thought of Edmund Winter and his family. Three days after their departure, the Tory Captain Coulson had arrived in the harbor in his new ship to take on his cargo of masts. But a group of angry townsmen had floated the masts up the river, well out of the captain's reach. Feelings against the Tories had risen to new heights, and Katharine was thankful that the Winter family had departed precipitantly on Michael's advice.

Michael himself had been gone nearly a month. Leaving his practice in the hands of Doctor Coffin, on June 10 he had set out for Cambridge to locate a cousin, the only living relative of the Smith children. From Falmouth to Cambridge was a distance of over a hundred miles; probably he had been four or five days on the road. But he could easily have arrived in time to take part in the battle fought on June 17 between British troops and rebels at a place called Breed's Hill. With a shudder she recalled the bloody descriptions of the engagement that Ben had picked up from one or two townsmen. The fact that there had been no word from Michael worried her. Ben reported that a young Doctor Warren, fighting on the rebel side, had been killed. Might not Michael also have played a part in the conflict?

Over the rim of the washtub Rachel's dark eyes regarded her anxiously. "We'll have to make more soap soon, ma'am," she suggested gently. "We have only a few bars left."

Katharine drew a deep breath and brought herself back to the tasks at hand. Except for Jonathan, who fell into mischief like a puppy unless he was watched constantly, the children worked as hard as she did. And they were far more competent, she admitted with a

sigh. Last evening Ben had made a roaring fire of maple
sticks in the brick oven, and while this was heating,
Rachel mixed the bread dough and set it to rise on the
hearth. After supper, when the walls of the oven were
deeply hot, Ben scraped the embers out, closed the flue,
and spread green leaves on the oven floor. Rachel took
up the "peel," which to the older girl looked like a flat
wooden shovel, sprinkled a little corn meal on it so that
the bread dough wouldn't stick, and placing the loaves
on it, thrust the peel into the oven, twitching the
loaves off onto the leaves. Withdrawing the shovel, she
sealed the front opening as tightly as possible. This
morning she had taken out the bread—crusty, brown,
and delicious.

Katharine had prepared their breakfast of corn mush
and molasses while Rachel dressed Jonathan. And afterward, while she had scoured the pewter bowls and mugs,
Rachel and Jonathan had fed the pig and scattered corn
to the chickens. Before breakfast Ben had milked the
cow. Afterward he had stacked the woodpile, filled the
heavy kettles with rain water for the wash, and toted
a bucket of drinking water from the well. Now he had
gone fishing. What he caught in the bay would be the
mainstay of their dinner.

Meeting Rachel's troubled glance, the older girl
smiled reassuringly as she scrubbed the clothes. "We'll
make the soap tomorrow," she promised, assuming a
confidence she did not feel. "Now, how about a song?"

Rachel loved to sing, and Katharine had begun to

teach her one or two of the old Scottish ballads she had
learned as a child. Together they began:

> *"It was in and about the Martinmas time,*
> *When the green leaves were a-fallin',*
> *That Sir John Graeme, in the West Country,*
> *Fell in love with Barbara Allan."*

As they sang on through the stanzas of *Barbara Allan*,
the wringing of the wash seemed to go more quickly.
Earlier, in her zeal to wring everything thoroughly,
Katharine had raised great blisters on her palms. Now
she put her vigor into the ballad.

They hung the wash in the sunshine and emptied the
heavy tubs. Then they released Jonathan, tied igno-
miniously to an apple tree out of harm's way. It was
madness, of course, to take him berrying, but there was
no one else to watch him, and she could not bear to
confine him again. They found the wild strawberries in
the field beyond the orchard plentiful and ripe. By the
time she and Rachel had picked all the berries, it was
noon. Jonathan's fair head drooped over his berry-
stained chin. Katharine carried him to the house, while
Rachel brought the laden baskets.

In the yard Ben was cleaning the fish he had caught.

"Cunners," he explained with a friendly grin.
"They're sweet, but full of bones."

"Then I'll give Jonathan bread and milk," Katharine
decided.

A few minutes later Jonathan was tucked into the trundle bed in the small chamber he shared with his brother. Even as she looked down at him, his eyes closed in sleep.

That afternoon she and Rachel took turns stirring and skimming the sticky mixture of strawberries and sugar in a kettle over the fire. Though the brew smelled delicious, it was hot work, and innumerable times she looked to Rachel for the signal to stop.

"It has to be just the right consistency," Rachel explained.

"But how do you know when it *is?*"

Rachel frowned. "You never do really," she confessed.

Finally the jam was in the pots, and they ran exploratory fingers round the edges of the kettle.

"Umm. It tastes good anyway." Katharine laughed with relief and picked up a wooden spoon. "Let's scoop up this little extra bit and give it to Ben."

Jonathan, bright-eyed and refreshed from his nap, went with them to the garden. At the edge, he and Rachel settled down in the grass, the girl tossing a yarn ball which the baby scrambled for with unflagging zeal. Ben was thinning the rows of carrots. Gathering up her skirts, Katharine walked carefully between the feathery rows, and held out the dollop of jam.

"Good!" Ben licked his lips in appreciation before he fell back again to his work. Katharine tossed the spoon to the grass and joined him.

She had never known such summer days as these, she reflected, easing a sliver of carrot out of the earth and dropping it on the pile near Ben. In England the air was softer, less intense. Here the days could be hot and humid, or bright and beautiful with cool, chill nights, and a wind from the sea. And after a rain everything was green and sparkling in its freshness. With a shudder she recalled the heavy, putrid dampness of Newgate, and she held up her face a moment to the hot, bright sun.

At supper they ate the tiny, rootlike carrots, for under Rachel's watchful eye nothing was ever wasted. Flour, sugar, salt, and molasses were the only staples the child ever willingly bought, Katharine had discovered, marveling at her excellent management.

When Jonathan was safely in bed and the chores were done, they settled before the fire, for the July evening had turned cold, a damp fog swirling about the house. As usual, Ben brought Katharine the family Bible.

"What shall it be tonight?" she asked.

"The Story of Ruth," Rachel pleaded.

"David and Goliath," Ben declared.

"I think we have time for both, but tonight, Rachel, will you begin, please?" Giving the Bible to Rachel, she took up one of Ben's shirts and began to mend a rent in a sleeve. The children badly needed to practice their reading, Katharine had discovered. Almost all of Rachel's schooling had been in the practical arts of sewing and cooking. And Ben was an impatient scholar at best.

Rachel began slowly, stumbling over the biblical

names. On the hearth her brother squirmed, but Katharine sent the girl an encouraging smile, and on the strength of this, Rachel plunged on to the end of the first chapter. Breathless and triumphant, she handed the Bible to Katharine, who finished reading The Book of Ruth.

The story of David and Goliath presented no problems. Ben knew the words almost by heart. It was evident as he read that, for the moment at least, Ben had become David, slayer of giants.

Katharine's mind drifted away from the story as she sewed on the last of the many silver buttons she had purchased from Mrs. Mosely to decorate the front of Michael's coat. They gave a handsome touch and they were genuine—an extravagance she could not really afford, but one that gave her great pleasure. Thrusting the coat at arm's length, she studied it doubtfully. Would it fit? She had patterned it after Michael's best black, which had hung in his closet in King Street. She had hoped to try it on him, willing to reveal the surprise to secure a perfect fit. But their last meetings had been so constrained—she herself painfully self-conscious in her efforts to measure up to his standards, Michael as stiffly formal as if he had been a stranger—that she could not introduce the coat. It was beautiful, she saw with pride. She was not yet ready to present it, however. His words still rankled in her heart, and she could not forget them. Until she had proved herself, until she stood exonerated in his eyes, she would make no gifts, she vowed to herself—no matter if it took all summer for Michael to recognize her worth.

When Ben had finished reading, he put the Bible carefully away on a shelf. While he banked the fire, Katharine checked the doors. Then they all climbed the stairs, murmuring good nights on the narrow landing. In the luminous dark of the small chamber they shared, Katharine and Rachel undressed and crept into bed. Almost at once they were asleep.

The making of soap, Katharine discovered the next day, was an arduous task. The fats in the kettle, placed over an outdoor fire, must be constantly stirred; the fumes from the lye rose in stinging waves, and after day-long labor the amount of soap seemed discouragingly small.

"It won't last very long, I fear," she said to Rachel with a weary shrug.

"No," Rachel agreed. "But we can always make some more."

The older girl felt a prick of shame. Surely, if discouragement were justified, it was Rachel who should complain! The child had no time for play, except for moments of keeping Jonathan amused, yet she never protested. And it had been Rachel today who had sung as they worked.

Impulsively she caught Rachel to her. "Someday you and I shall have a holiday," she promised.

That evening, after the children were in bed, she stayed up to work the second stocking of a pair that would encompass Jonathan's plump legs come winter. The days were simply not long enough for all that there was to do. As she knitted and purled in the light of a single candle, her brain schemed for a means of getting into the house on King Street. Rachel had nothing to put on her back but her workgown and one other made up from calico Katharine herself had purchased for her from Mrs. Mosely at an exorbitant price. The child's winter wardrobe, she had discovered in dismay, consisted of a single faded frock, twice-turned and much too small. Already she had cut up Mrs. Winter's heavy black gown to make a cloak for Rachel. But if Annette's closet held any of her old clothes, how welcome they would be! She longed, too, to get her hands on some books for Ben. *Robinson Crusoe, The Pilgrim's Progress,* the plays of Shakespeare—these could be a happy supplement to the stories of the Old Testament in the long winter evenings to come.

A knock on the door startled her, and she answered hesitantly. "Who—who is it?"

"Michael."

Katharine jumped up, slid back the bolt, and opened the door to him.

Shadowed, lean, he stood looking down at her, and seeing him again, she felt a flood of gladness sweep her heart.

"Are you well?" His hands were tight round her own. She nodded.

"And the children?"

"They seem to thrive on hard work." She led him to a chair, and in the light of the candle studied him more closely. His face was darkly tanned, his brown eyes direct and intent. "Oh, Michael!" she cried, impetuously grasping his arm. "I am so glad that you are safely back!" And then, recalling similar impulsive words to Edmund Winter, she blushed and sat down in confusion. Snatching up the sock, she applied herself industriously to it. "When did you return?" she asked primly.

"About an hour ago."

"Oh." Katharine was both vexed and flattered. "Surely after such a long journey, you could have waited till morning to see us?"

"Perhaps. But I did not."

"Have you eaten?"

"Enough." Stretching his legs, he leaned back in the chair. "You will be happy to learn that I have found the cousin," he said with a smile.

"Tell me," she urged.

"Before she died, Rebecca Smith told me that she had a cousin living in Cambridge somewhere near a tavern. That helped me locate the house. I found Mrs. Bradley—she is a woman somewhat over thirty—with no difficulty. Her husband was not at home on the day I arrived—he is a tanner by trade—for he had joined the Massachusetts militia. After the battle with the British on Breed's Hill, I dressed a bayonet wound in his side, though I did not know at the time who he was."

"Then you were in that terrible fight!" she exclaimed. "I feared you might be!"

He shook his head. "No, I did not take part in it. But I saw most of it, and I did what I could afterward, of course. It will be some time before Amos Bradley fully recovers, and I doubt if he will fight again. When I returned to Cambridge a day or so after the battle, I realized how serious a wound he had sustained. I thought it wise to remain in Cambridge until he was out of danger. That is why I have been gone so long. But you will like them, Katharine. Both he and his wife are good countrypeople. They want very much to come here and care for the children. They themselves are childless."

"Could he find work here?"

"A good tanner can always find work. Cotton could probably use him in his tannery on Fore Street."

"And does she seem a good woman, Michael?"

"Yes, I believe her to be as fine a person as her husband. And he is a man of good sense and sound principles."

"Ah." Katharine gave a happy sigh.

"There is one drawback." Michael rose and went to the window, tracing an outline on the black pane. "As things are, I do not believe they can get here before the middle of October." He swung round to face her. "It was not—is not—my intention that you be housekeeper here all that time."

Katharine raised her head. "Oh?"

"Before she sailed my aunt told me that you had refused a position in New York to honor your promise to me. Believe me, I am grateful. The position may still be open, however, and even if it is not, New York is filled with Tory families, many of them well to do, quite able to hire you at a good wage. Now that I am here, you are free to leave Falmouth at any time, of course."

A quiver of anger ran through her. How dare he assume so much!

With an effort she controlled her voice. "And if I choose to stay here?"

"Stay here?" he repeated incredulously.

"Yes."

"I do not believe I understand you, Katharine." Crossing the room, he came to stand beside her, regarding her with a puzzled frown. "Once you told me— quite emphatically, as I recall—that you wanted comfort and security." His voice took on a dry note. "Surely you find neither here!"

She shrugged, finding for some reason a perverse delight in his perplexity. "Nevertheless," she said firmly, "I should like to remain here, at least until the cousins come."

For a long moment he was silent, staring down at her. He seemed at last to accept her decision, for he spoke of something else.

"I have been concerned for you these past weeks," he said slowly, almost in apology. "There is so little money."

"Yes," she murmured. "I know."

She waited, but Michael apparently did not intend to admit to supporting the family. She herself would have been unaware of his help had not Rachel confided that the reason for her strict economy was her determination to take as little from the doctor's funds as possible.

"I believe Rachel keeps all of the family fortune in that tea caddy on the shelf," she offered, pointing to the place.

He went to the shelf and got down the tea chest, rummaging in it. "Ah, you've done better than I expected," he exclaimed in admiration. "When I left, there was not too much more than what is here now."

Katharine nodded, amused and touched at Michael's reluctance to admit his own generosity. "Rachel is in charge," she explained, coming to her feet and shaking out her gown. "You must give her the credit for good management."

"I do." He replaced the tea caddy and swung round to face her. "But she did not do it alone." Crossing to her, he lifted one of her hands and ran a gentle finger over the callus on her palm. "Believe me, I honor you for your part, too."

"Thank you," she murmured, moved by his earnestness.

He was gone a moment later, and she climbed the stairs to bed.

Out of pride and pique she had been goaded into coming here, she reflected, as she undressed and crept into bed. Her only desire had been to prove herself to Michael. But Ben's sturdy spirit, Rachel's quiet strength, and Jonathan's loving acceptance had won her heart. Now she served them gladly. And she served Michael, too, she thought with a wry pleasure for which she could not fully account. Every household penny saved was gold in Michael's pocket. He could refuse her offer of passage money, but he could hardly know if she supplemented the funds in the tea caddy with an occasional coin of her own. With a little smile of triumph, Katharine fell asleep.

17

As the July days waxed hot and full, the garden came on in abundance. Peas and lettuce replaced asparagus. August brought beans, beets, carrots, cucumbers, and corn. But time, Katharine found, the most precious commodity of all, winged away as she and Rachel struggled to store up as much as possible for the winter months. Peas, beans, and corn were dried. Cucumbers in crocks of brine and bags of carrots, onions, and beets were placed in the dry cellar under the house.

In the early autumn Ben dug the potatoes, and they sorted out the firm ones, setting aside for early use those the fork had bruised. Cabbage and squash and apples were picked and stored.

Frost came, and now in early October with the

harvest in, Ben returned to his classes at the grammar school. But his heart was not in his studies.

"I want to go to sea," he confided to Katharine, as she prepared apples to be dried.

"Then the study of mathematics will be helpful to you, Ben."

"But if I could ship out as a cabin boy—" Ben's eyes were dreamy.

She was in sympathy with his dreams. "Someday, perhaps, you can go to sea," she answered gently, knowing full well that Ben was realist enough to recognize that now he had no choice. Young as he was, the man's work of the family fell to him.

The days grew cooler. Then one morning in early October the air was again balmy under a gentle breeze, and a brilliant sun moved up the sky.

"An Indian summer's day," Rachel told Katharine as they burnished the newly scrubbed floor with sand. As she spoke, the shaft of sunlight streaming through the open doorway was broken. Katharine looked up.

"Michael!" she exclaimed, rising quickly.

"Good morning! Dare we venture onto this magnificent floor?" Michael ushered an old woman in a rusty-black gown and bonnet into the room. "Mrs. Nolan, may I present Mistress Katharine and Mistress Rachel, after yourself the two finest housekeepers in all Falmouth?"

The girls curtsied, and the old woman chuckled, her

toothless face a mass of wrinkles squeezing her eyes into pale green slits.

"And Master Jonathan!" With a swoop Michael gathered up Jonathan, whose clenched fists leaked streams of sand.

"I am declaring a holiday," the doctor continued. "Mrs. Nolan has consented to stay with Jonathan while the rest of us go for a sail." He handed Jonathan to the widow. "Quick now, before she changes her mind!" The girls sped toward the stairs. "And bring cloaks," Michael shouted after them. "The wind may change!"

Katharine scrambled into her old gown of gray linen, worn but fresh, while Rachel donned her summer calico, snatching up her cloak and Katharine's as if a moment's delay might mean the end of this delightful treat. Matching Michael's strides, they arrived at the wharf a few minutes later, where to Katharine's surprise, Ben awaited them.

In answer to her inquiring glance, Michael grinned.

"The schoolmaster is a friend of mine," he said blandly, and joined in her laughter.

She had never sailed in so small a boat, and found herself suddenly alive to the exhilarating joy of slicing through blue water whose spray touched her face to dampness and curled back her hair like a pony's mane.

"It's like sleighing!" she cried in delight to Michael, who sat opposite with Rachel. Ben was at the tiller, his brown eyes bright with joy.

They anchored in a small cove of one of the many

islands in Casco Bay. Ben rowed the girls ashore in the dingy, and then returned for Michael.

"Could we take off our shoes and stockings?" Rachel asked. "Ben and Doctor Edes will."

Katharine agreed, finding the sand deliciously warm beneath her bare feet.

While Michael and Ben searched for flat rocks, the two girls gathered driftwood. At last they had enough. Michael now knelt to hollow out a hole in the sand. With the flat rocks he lined the bottom of this shallow pit, then carefully fitted other rocks along the sides. Placing some of the driftwood in this rock oven, he kindled a fire. Ben, meantime, gathered up an armful of seaweed and dropped it down on the sand.

"The stones won't heat up for some time," Michael said to the children. "If you want to explore, go ahead."

They drifted off along the beach.

Katharine looked at the fire. "Why are you heating the rocks?" she asked curiously.

"We have lobsters in that sack." He pointed. "When the fire dies down, the rocks will be very hot. A layer of seaweed, the lobsters, some more seaweed—believe me, they will be cooked fit for a king. No," he amended with a smile, "far too good for the present incumbent on the throne."

Stretching out beside her on the sand, he lay with his face to the sun, the lazy strength of his lean body relaxed. How comfortable he is to be with, Katharine thought, regarding the shabby breeches and worn shirt with more charity than usual. Scooping up a handful of sand, she let it sift through her fingers. The sun, the sea, and the intoxicating warmth bemused her, and she said contentedly, "This is a lovely spot, Michael. Everything is so safe and secure."

He laughed. "It only appears to be. In a winter storm you would find it rough indeed. It is much like the rest of the world. There is no real safety anywhere."

She watched the sand dribble out of her palm, a little frown gathering on her forehead. "Why do you say that?" she asked slowly.

Turning, he looked up at her, a quizzical expression in his eyes. "You know history as well as I do. Who was ever secure? A prince? A pauper? A kitchenmaid? A queen? Neither the palace nor the cottage can stem the tide of poverty, of war, of disease, and of death."

She was silent, knowing he spoke the truth, and feeling it fall like a great shadow across the beauty of this day.

"What security there is," he went on bluntly, "lies within yourself—in your hands or in your head. And you create it by hard work—and heartbreaking labor it can be sometimes." Pulling himself up, he looked out over the green water. "If you are a woman, you spin and weave, cook and scrub, bear children"—his voice grew harsh for a moment—"and sometimes give your life in the process. If you are a man, you are seaman, teacher, physician—doing as good a job as you know how."

"And—and is this all?" Dismay tinged her voice. For

he had mentioned none of the gentler things—the warmth of a candlelit room, the pleasure of music, the joy of books, the delight in a new gown. He had ignored the creature comforts that money could purchase, and to Katharine he seemed to have cut existence down to nothing but the bitter striving for daily bread.

"No, this is not quite all," he said reflectively. "When a man loves his work and gives his whole heart to it, he achieves a kind of satisfaction. And when a woman devotes herself to the welfare of others, she, too, is rewarded." He looked up and met her eyes. "You have proved that these last months, have you not?" he asked with a smile. For a long moment his gaze rested on her, then he looked back to the sea. When he spoke again, his words came more slowly. "But when there is mutual devotion, a deep and abiding love between a man and a woman, then, I think, there can be a contentment that comes close to the security you dream of. This is true happiness, perhaps."

She was silent. With a careful hand she smoothed a circle in the sand, pondering his words, trying to clarify her own dreams. For the image of happiness she held now was not the one she had forged in prison out of anger and despair. There, with a kind of desperate frenzy, she had longed for gold—enough, at least, to secure her freedom. Once free, she had fancied herself mistress of Edmund Winter's house, secure in the luxury and comfort of King Street. How distant and childish such a dream seemed today! Yet she could not readily define just what it was she was searching for now, she thought with a prick of uneasiness. She, too, had experienced the gratification of a job well done. Her success with Ben, Rachel, and Jonathan warmed her heart like a flame. Yet she knew that this was not all she wanted. There was a deeper longing.

Rejecting this disturbing speculation, Katharine turned to him, voicing now the question that was in every heart and on almost every tongue.

"How do you think this rebellion will end, Michael?" she asked in grave tones.

"Six months ago I would have said it was only a matter of time until the King's troops crushed every rebel," he replied. "Now—well, I think we have a chance. I saw some of the fighting at Breed's Hill, you recall—the Battle of Bunker Hill, men call it now." He fell silent, brooding, as he tossed a couple of sticks into the rock oven. Then he glanced up, and she saw his eyes bright with excitement. "Everything came clear for me that day, Katharine! Against the bravest troops in the world, the British regulars, our militia men under Colonel Prescott—farmers, mostly, in leather trousers and homespun coats—stood and fought. Not for money or for fame, or because they were too disciplined to run —they fought for a cause. And despite their incredible courage, the King's troops were slaughtered. They were killed by men willing to stand against bayonets—men who themselves had no more powder, and held nothing in their hands but empty muskets."

Katharine shuddered, seeing in her mind's eye the scarlet-clad bodies of the royal troops, broken and scattered on the hillside.

" 'We have a chance,' " she quoted uneasily. Was Michael now fully committed to the rebel cause?

"Yes." He answered her unspoken question. "I count myself one of them, a patriot—a rebel, if you will—though I did nothing that day but bind up the wounds of braver men, and deserve no credit for the victory."

Katharine looked at him in consternation. "But Michael!" she cried, flinging out her hands in a gesture of entreaty. "The rebels have no money, no ammunition, no leaders—*theirs is a losing cause!*"

He faced her squarely. "When he arrived in Cambridge in early July to take command of the troops, I saw General Washington. He is a giant of a man—big in stature and possessed of great dignity." For a moment he paused, searching for the exact words he wanted. "And he has something else," he said slowly. "I would call it integrity. Believe me, he commands respect. Men will follow him."

"One man!" she scoffed, unwilling to attribute such virtues to any rebel leader, and shaken by Michael's earnestness.

"It may take only one man—if he is big enough." Abruptly he stood up. "Before the end of October I myself shall leave for Cambridge to join the army. I have been offered a commission, and I shall serve as a surgeon."

"Oh, Michael," she whispered, feeling her last bulwark being swept away.

"The children's cousins arrive next week," he said brusquely. "They will be in good hands. I can see you safely to Cambridge, and from there make arrangements for you to go on to New York."

His voice was cool and restrained, and to Katharine it seemed that he had already detached himself from his old life, and all that remained now was to be rid of her. And why not, she thought bitterly. Michael had aligned himself with the rebel cause. Now she was an enemy.

18

On the sixteenth of October, Amos Bradley and his wife Deborah arrived in Falmouth, having traveled overland from Cambridge. Scrutinizing this unknown cousin with the wary eye of a mother hen, Katharine could find no fault with her. Small, plump, modestly gowned in gray homespun, her worn satin bonnet framed a gentle face that grew radiant at the sight of Rachel and Jonathan. She loves children, the girl thought, with a surge of thankfulness.

"We have looked forward to your coming, ma'am." Taking her cloak and bonnet, she led their guest to a chair.

"We came as soon as my husband's wound would allow him to travel comfortably." Deborah Bradley smiled as she looked around the tiny parlor. "But where is Ben?" she asked.

"Ben is at school, ma'am," Rachel answered softly, standing a little to one side.

"Of course." Her friendly smile embraced Rachel, who came a little closer, Jonathan clinging to one hand. Deborah Bradley regarded Jonathan with the same frank interest he exhibited in her. "Do you think he might let me hold him?" she asked, putting out her arms.

Jonathan plumped willingly into his cousin's lap, absorbed immediately in a string of spools she drew from her bag.

"You must tell me everything he eats or does not eat," she said with a smile at Katharine, her hand smoothing Jonathan's silky hair. "I have much to learn about babies, I fear."

"You will find Rachel a great help to you, ma'am." Katharine gave Rachel's hand a little squeeze, feeling her own heart contract. How she would miss Rachel's steadfast devotion!

Amos Bradley came in now, having circled the outside of the house, "to get his bearings," he said, although Katharine suspected his tardy appearance had been previously arranged to give his wife time to get acquainted. Big and friendly, he walked with a slight limp, but his gaze was clear and his handclasp firm. Katharine liked him. He looked strong and capable.

Ben appeared after school to greet his relatives. And now in the late afternoon, Katharine found herself pulling on her cloak, catching Jonathan to her in a swift hug, and trying not to see the tears in Rachel's eyes as Ben carried her bag down the stairs. Since the little dwelling could house only one mistress, she would spend the next few days as Michael's guest, under the Widow Nolan's chaperonage.

As soon as they were free of the house, Ben exploded with the news he was carrying.

"The *Canseaux* came into the harbor today!" he announced.

"You mean Captain Mowat? Why should he return?" Katharine asked incredulously.

Ben shook his head. "No one seems to know. He's got a supply ship with him, as well as two schooners and a bomb sloop."

"Ben!" She stopped short, staring at him. "*Five ships?*"

"Yes. I suppose he means to steal some of the cattle and sheep that are kept on the islands—the hay, too, perhaps."

"But he can't do that!" she protested. "That hay and cattle belong to the people of Falmouth!"

"Fresh meat would taste pretty good to the men on those ships," Ben said briefly. "And who's to stop him?" He shifted her bag to his other hand. "Though I did hear someone say that some men from the militia companies have been sent over to the islands to stand guard."

Katharine was silent. What right had a King's captain

to seize cattle and sheep not belonging to him? Unless he meant to pay for them, of course.

"Perhaps he intends to buy the supplies," she suggested hopefully.

Ben sent her a sardonic glance. "Do you really think so?"

"No," she admitted.

They had reached the doctor's house, and Ben unlatched the gate. Although she had passed the house several times when she and the children had gone berrying, Katharine had never been inside. Now, the Widow Nolan, taciturn and frowning, opened the door, guiding the boy up the steep, narrow stairs that led abruptly out of the entryway. Ben dropped the bag in the room Mrs. Nolan indicated. Katharine thanked him and he sped away.

"If ye want me, ye'll find me in the kitchen," the widow announced with asperity.

Hearing the old woman's determined descent of the stairs, the girl smiled a little ruefully to herself. Obviously she was not welcome. Well, it was only for a few days.

From her bag she lifted the blue muslin gown, limp and worn now. Yet how beautiful it had seemed that first night out of prison! The rose wool, Edmund's gift, and the long blue shawl came next. Then she drew out Michael's coat. Tonight she would give it to him, she resolved happily. Pride had prevented her presenting the gift until she felt she had proved herself. But

Michael's own glance these last few days told her that she stood exonerated in his eyes.

Downstairs Mrs. Nolan received her offer of help with a negative shake of her head.

" 'Tis I gets Doctor Edes's supper," she said dourly, emphasizing again that in her eyes Katharine was an intruder, to be borne but not embraced.

When at last Michael arrived, darkness had fallen.

"Are you securely established above?" His smile made her feel welcome for the first time since she had entered the house.

"I am not quite sure," she murmured, sending a wary glance at the widow's back, and wondering wryly if the bones she had encountered in her bowl of fish chowder had been deliberately inserted.

He said nothing but gave her a broad wink.

After supper the old woman banged the pewter plates into their cupboard, and then thumped up the stairs to her chamber. Katharine suppressed a giggle, and Michael grinned.

"She accepts no one at face value," he explained. "It took me a month to prove my worth. Tell me, what do you think of my dwelling?"

"Oh, Michael! It is a dear little house!" she exclaimed. Then, hearing the words, excited and overloud, she bit her tongue. Had she sounded condescending?

"Come and see my surgery." He opened a door off the kitchen, and held the candle high to reveal a small room, starkly whitewashed. Two straight-backed chairs and a long table were the only furnishings, except for numerous bottles and jars against one wall. Bunches of dried herbs dangled from one corner of the ceiling. One or two books lay on a chair.

Michael looked at the books and sighed. "Each day I mean to get a permit from the Committee to allow me to go into Edmund's house and pick up my other books. And each day something more important seems to claim my attention. Well, they are safe there, I trust. Though I would hate to lose them, for books are harder to come by every day now." He turned back to her. "Do you like it?"

She nodded. "And does that door lead outdoors?"

"Yes. My patients can pull a bell that sounds in the kitchen. But I care for them here."

They returned to the fire. As she took up one of her second-best gloves to darn a worn finger, she related Ben's news of the ships in the harbor.

"They have set the whole town in a toss," Michael agreed. "And Ben is right. Fresh meat would taste very good to those men aboard. They're having the devil's own time victualing the ships in Boston—and no doubt Mowat has come from there." Poking at the fire, he brought up its blaze. "Those seamen lead wretched lives —never enough to eat, and the rags on their backs bought out of their own pay. God knows that's little enough."

His words gave her the excuse she was looking for.

Katharine jumped up. "I'll only be a moment," she assured him.

Candle in hand, she hurried up the stairs to her chamber. Over a chair lay Michael's coat. She took it up, and holding the candle carefully lest the wax drip on the material, she started down the stairs. For a moment her heart misgave her. Michael would resent the suggestion of any payment of her debt to him. She must be very careful how she presented the gift. Her eyes came back to the coat, and she looked at it with new pride. How handsome it was! The silver buttons gleamed and the heavy braid at the wrists gave it an air of quiet elegance.

She drew up on the threshold. "Close your eyes!" she commanded breathlessly.

He turned his back to her, a bent arm covering his face. "Is it a surprise?"

She laughed. "Yes! And you must take off your coat!"

"Good heavens! Shall I kneel also, O Queen?"

"That will not be necessary." Katharine tried to be prim, but inwardly she was trembling with excitement.

Flinging off his coat, he turned to her, and she thrust the gift into his hands.

"Ah." His fingers caressed the cloth. "It is indeed regal," he said softly. Then his brown eyes, bright with pleasure, met hers. "It is quite the handsomest present anyone has ever bestowed on me. I thank you, ma'am."

"Try it on," she begged.

Pulling the coat on, he thrust back his shoulders and stood stiffly erect. She circled him in frowning concentration, noting the fit of the shoulders and the length of the sleeves.

"How—how do you feel?"

"Like a bridegroom."

"Michael! Be serious." Katharine looked at him pleadingly. "Does it fit?"

"I *am* serious." He smiled down at her. "And it does fit—perfectly, as you see."

With a happy sigh she sank into her chair.

He swept her a bow. "Am I to understand, madam, that this is a token of your esteem?"

"Yes." She nodded, her eyes and mind still happily absorbed in her handwork. "And of my gratitude," she added, oblivious of her words.

She saw him stiffen and knew too late her error. Meeting hers, his eyes grew dark with anger, and he spoke curtly, his words coming in a hard, level tone. "We have had this out before, Katharine," he said coldly. "You owe me nothing." Wrenching off the coat, he flung it in her lap. "And God knows," he added harshly, "I do not want your *gratitude!*"

For an instant she was speechless. Then fury spurred her to her feet. How dare he fling down a gift she had made so lovingly, bestowed with such pride? Clutching up the coat, she stood before him, white with anger.

"Does the reason for a gift make such—such a difference?" Her voice broke on the question, and to her consternation she burst into helpless tears.

"Katharine!" The coat fell to the chair as he caught

up her hands and drew her close. "I beg your pardon! The reason does not matter—at least to no one else. Forgive me, I beg. I have no right to demand explanations of your generosity to me." On her hair she felt his hand, gentle in its touch, and despite her hurt, she was overwhelmed with a sudden, incongruous longing to stay within his arms. But pride, sweeping up in hot, angry waves, drowned this impulse, and withdrawing from him, she turned sharply away.

"We are both weary, I fear." There was resignation in his voice, and she heard his sigh. He said no more, but going to the hearth, took up the broom and swept the ashes of the fire into a gray mound that would harbor a flame until morning. Then, lifting the candle, he lighted her up the stairs.

At the door of her chamber he halted. "You will find extra blankets, should you need them, in the small trunk in your room. My aunt managed to get both woolens and silver out of the reach of the Committee and into this house, and to do it with neither my knowledge nor consent," he said somewhat dryly. Opening the door into her room, he crossed to the bedside table and held the flame of his candle to the wick of hers till it burst into flame. "There is no need for you to rise early tomorrow," he said in a quiet, matter-of-fact tone. "Unless, of course, you wish to." He bowed good night.

How sensitive he was, she thought, as she undressed and got into bed, feeling again a burning indignation— how proud and stubborn! Why must their rare moments together end so often in misunderstanding or strife? Yet, in that brief respite within the shelter of his arms, she had known a contentment so deep and encompassing that recalling it now her heart quickened in a yearning she knew was dangerously close to love. What was she thinking of! To dream of Michael would be the height of folly, she told herself angrily. Generous and charming he could be, handsome he certainly was, but these gentlemanly attributes were founded on solid New England convictions, the very core of his devotion to a cause she heartily despised.

In the morning she rose late. Reluctant to interrupt Mrs. Nolan's schedule, she did not take breakfast, but spent the half hour before noon examining the house more closely. With their dormer windows set in the slanting roof, the chambers were snug and cozy; patchwork quilts covered the canopied beds; braided rugs stretched across the wide floor boards. Downstairs, the tiny parlor held a few books, a walnut table against one wall, two wing chairs beside the hearth, and a handsome pine desk in one corner. But like most New England houses, it was the kitchen that reflected the life of the household, and she entered it now to find a fire blazing in the enormous fireplace, and the fragrance of fresh bread filling the air.

"Doctor's been called away for a lying-in." Mrs. Nolan greeted her brusquely as she scoured a pan. "Gone to Windham, eleven miles or more. May not be back till tomorrow." She waved Katharine to a chair. "Ye'll have to wait on yerself."

Katharine poured out a mugful of hot chocolate, and cut a slice of the new bread.

"He doesn't have much time to enjoy his new home, does he?" she asked, biting into the brown crust.

"No." The widow shook her head. "If ye ask me, he'll get more rest in the army."

As the afternoon advanced, the girl found her new leisure wearisome. The house was appallingly quiet, and it seemed somehow in Michael's absence to take on the dour complexion of its housekeeper. Pulling on her cloak she escaped out-of-doors into the bright October sunshine.

She strolled down Back Street and turned into King. Always here her spirits revived, for the street was impressively reassuring with its captains' and merchants' homes reflecting a smug respectability. If Michael would only remain in practice here in Falmouth, he, too, could soon purchase a more imposing home. But he would scorn such an idea. He was without worldly ambition, and esteem—other than the respect accorded him as a competent physician—meant nothing to him, she acknowledged with regret.

She was aware suddenly of a large crowd of men and women converging at the corner of King and Middle Streets. Hurrying up, Katharine accosted a townswoman.

"What is going on?" she asked curiously.

"A little while ago Captain Mowat sent an officer on shore with a letter for the Committee," the woman replied shortly. "They say it'll be read out to us any moment now."

As she spoke, a man came out to stand on the steps of the new County House. He waved a letter in his hand, and some of the murmuring died down.

"This letter comes from Captain Mowat aboard His Majesty's Ship *Canseaux*. The *Canseaux* is anchored out there in the harbor," he added laconically, "with four other King's ships."

An angry muttering greeted this announcement, and Katharine, on the edge of the crowd, could not hear the opening words of Captain Mowat's address to the townspeople. But suddenly absolute quiet descended, and the words came clear and harsh:

". . . in place of a dutiful and grateful return to your King and parent State, you have been guilty of the most unpardonable rebellion, supported by the ambition of a set of designing men, whose insidious deeds have cruelly imposed on the credulity of their fellow creatures, and at last have brought the whole into the same dilemma; which leads me to feel not a little the woes of the innocent of them, in particular on the present occasion, from my having it in Orders to execute a just punishment on the town of Falmouth. In the name of which authority I previously warn you to remove without delay the human species out of the said town, for which purpose I give you the time of two hour; at the period of which, a red pendant will be hoisted at the main top gallant mast head, with a gun. But should your imprudence lead you to show the least resistance, you will in that case free me of that humanity so strongly pointed out in my Orders, as well as in my inclination.

"I do also observe that all those who did on a former occasion fly to the King's ship under my command for protection, that the same door is now open to receive them.

"The Officer who will deliver this letter I expect to return immediately unmolested.

"I am,

    H. Mowat, Captain."

A man beside her spoke in slow, unbelieving tones. "By God, he means to lay the town in ashes!" Looking up, his eyes met Katharine's, and she recognized him as one of the seamen who had been aboard the *Claire* on her voyage from London. "Miss Leslie!" He gave her a polite bow, but his words were barbed. "You'll fly to the King's ship, no doubt, like a good Tory!"

"I shall seek no refuge from a tyrant such as this!" Katharine flared, outraged at the letter and its tone.

She stayed only long enough to see three men appointed to wait upon Captain Mowat in the hope of coming to terms and somehow preventing the town's destruction.

Spreading like a flame, the alarming news outstripped her in reaching Mrs. Nolan. She found the old woman trembling with a rage so violent it left her helpless.

"Where to begin," she muttered, moving aimlessly from room to room. "Where to begin?"

Swiftly Katharine took command. "Get me every bucket there is in the house, Mrs. Nolan," she ordered. "If we have only two hours before the ships begin to fire, there is not a moment to lose. We must draw as much water as we can from the well."

Every bucket, pan, and kettle was filled at last, and Katharine's arms ached with such agony she could have wept. But she was a little comforted. Water was a weapon, though how much or how little would be needed against the explosion of a shell, she dared not consider.

A banging of the knocker sent her flying to the door. Ben stood on the step.

"Captain Mowat's consented to postpone the bombardment till tomorrow morning," he gasped, as Katharine led him inside. "He says he will hold off, provided we deliver up some arms tonight. And he says he'll send an express to Admiral Graves in Boston asking for a postponement of his order to burn the town—provided the people will deliver up the cannon and all small arms and ammunition by eight o'clock tomorrow morning."

"Oh, Ben, then we are safe!" she cried in relief, sinking down on a chair.

"The town will never surrender all its arms!" Ben

looked at her in astonishment. "It would leave us with no protection at all!"

"Where are the men of the militia companies?"

"On the islands, guarding the cattle and hay. They were sent there earlier when everyone thought that was what Mowat was after. Some of them will come back when they hear of this threat. But they may not get here in time to be of any real help."

Katharine jumped up. "I know the town is a hotbed of rebels," she said fiercely. "But even so, no one, rebel or Tory, deserves to have his house burned down around his ears!"

As always, Ben came straight to the point. "We are at war now," he reminded her grimly.

"Yes," she admitted with reluctance, giving him a grateful hand. "You were good to come, Ben, and I thank you." Opening the front door to let him out, she choked on the cloud of dust raised by a passing oxcart. Already families were fleeing, their household goods piled on carts and wagons, as they made their way out of the town. Katharine looked at them doubtfully. "Will your family go into the country until it is over?"

Ben drew himself up. "We'll fight," he said with resolution. "My cousin Amos swears he'll kill any King's man who dares set foot across our threshold!"

With a shudder she closed the door. What madness this was! Did the King's ministers imagine for a moment that by measures such as these they would win the rebels to their side? Four or five armed ships would wreak havoc firing into a town whose every house was made of wood. How dare the King inflict such hardship? Not since her imprisonment had she felt a rage as passionate as this. Such vengeance on the helpless was as wickedly unjust as transporting Mary for stealing bread for her starving child—as cruelly unfair as her own harsh sentence. In renewed fury she paced across the small parlor. Then she drew up, aghast at her defiance. This was the thinking of a rebel!

After supper she and Mrs. Nolan wrapped Michael's most precious possessions in an old blanket and stowed them in a barrel in the cellar. What an irony, the girl reflected, that the china teapot trailing its gentle roses, the silver spoons and candelabra that had graced the table for the King's officers—indeed, all that Mrs. Winter had so carefully removed from the hands of the rebels must now be protected from the fire and flame of the King's own ships.

"I can think of no more we can do," she said at last with a weary sigh, lifting a grimy hand to her hair, a mass of cobwebs and dust. "If only Michael were here, he could guide us!"

"Babies take their own time comin'." Leading the way up the cellar stairs, Mrs. Nolan was philosophical. "And there may be other things keepin' him in Windham. With all them carts and wagons puttin' out for the country, he'll learn soon enough what a fix we're in!"

They continued on to the upstairs landing, where

the old woman paused a moment, holding her candle so that its gleam fell full on her companion's face.

"Ye're not good enough for him, ye know," she said tartly, giving Katharine a long glance. "But ye may be— in time."

In her bedchamber the girl pondered this cryptic judgment as she brushed the dust from her hair. Did Mrs. Nolan imagine that she had set her cap for Michael? The old housekeeper's words were ridiculously presumptuous. Yet she could not entirely dismiss them. Her feelings for Michael were not easily explained. This peculiar sense of frustration—so acute in his absence— how much did it mean? His maddening pride! Why did it rouse her to such wrath? And surely she should be able to ignore his cool appraisal of her motives and actions? Yet she responded not with a casual disregard for his opinions, but with a grim determination to prove herself. For, absurd though it was, she wanted his approval. Michael possessed a self-discipline and integrity she recognized and fully respected. Perhaps she did not deserve him, she acknowledged with a wry humility that left her uncomfortably aware of her own failings and bereft of her usual pride.

She would meet other men, she reflected sensibly, and with this consoling thought she settled into bed, determined to dismiss Michael from her mind. She did not need him. She was well able to stand alone. With Annette, had she not proved her worth as a teacher? And these last months under Rachel's loving eye she had mastered a dozen household arts. She could look after herself, she thought resolutely. And New York would be far larger and more civilized than this rebellious little New England town! Surely in New York, even within the restricted world of the governess, she would find her heart's desire.

But what *was* her heart's desire? Twisting beneath the quilts, Katharine realized with a shock that she was no longer sure. From this disquieting revelation, she wrenched her mind up short, experiencing a kind of panic as she forced herself to lie still. She closed her eyes, trying desperately to define her goals, but now, infuriatingly, Michael's kiss touched her again. And in the fitful slumber that finally claimed her, she roused to every nighttime noise, half-wondering if this were his step upon the stair.

19

The morning of October 18, 1775, in Falmouth, Maine, dawned clear and calm. From her chamber window Katharine looked out across the rooftops to the harbor below. The *Canseaux*, the *Cat*, and three other war-ships rode quietly at anchor. No wind stirred the sea, and beside the house the wrinkled leaves of an old oak hung limp. But though air and sea were quiet, the town was fully alive. A motley parade of animals and "human species" in Mowat's contemptuous term, crawled along Back Street, striving anxiously to escape into the coun-try out of range of the ships' guns. She watched a man in a patched homespun shirt and breeches goad his ox team, while his wife and children balanced precariously amid the feather beds, chairs, copper kettles, fire tongs, fur robes, barrels of apples, and other miscellany that made up the load. Atop a pile of clothing an orange cat huddled, and a collie ran alongside. On the tail of the wagon a small girl nestled a brown hen in the crook of her arm, her other hand clutching a beribboned bonnet, too precious to be worn, apparently. As the wagon lurched into a hole, a half dozen cabbages tumbled from it to the ditch, bumping among potatoes and pumpkins scattered by earlier drivers. Two small boys leapt from the load to retrieve the cabbages and stumbled back to the still-moving wagon, flinging themselves close to their sister. Over everything dust danced in golden flecks, reflecting the rays of the early sun.

A few minutes later Katharine was interrupted at breakfast by Ben.

"The Committee's back from the *Canseaux*," he announced breathlessly. "They told Captain Mowat the town would *not* surrender its cannon and arms. At nine o'clock the ships will open fire." He raced away to give the news to other families.

Mrs. Nolan shrugged beneath her shawl. "We're as near ready now for the villains' mischief as we ever will be," she said stoically. "Pray God the balls won't reach this far, or if they do, strike somewheres else."

Promptly at nine o'clock a trembling seized the little house, and a noise like thunder echoed over it. Katharine ran to an upstairs window. Whiffs of smoke curled over the gun ports of four of the ships, and even as she watched, more flame and smoke belched out. The burning of Falmouth had begun.

All day long the firing continued. By afternoon the view of the harbor was completely obscured by a pall of smoke that hung in a black cloud over the lower part of the town. The tower of St. Paul's Church flamed like a funeral pyre. And the carts passing now, the girl saw in pity and helpless rage, were goaded by frantic men, oblivious of their possessions, bent only on saving their families from the awful havoc of the ships' guns.

She dared not try to assist others; there was not time. One bursting shell could scatter fire in all directions, and the wooden shingles of the little house were dry as tinder. Already sparks from nearby dwellings had drifted onto the roof. Twice she climbed the oak and hung out on a branch to fling water on the fiery bits that seemed to descend like slow crimson stars from the sky. Lowering an empty bucket on a rope, she waited impatiently for Mrs. Nolan to slop more water into it, then hauled it laboriously up again. Her hands were blistered by the rope, and once she had nearly fallen. But with every spark extinguished she felt a stab of triumph against the spitting ships.

As the afternoon wore on, she had begun to think that by some miracle they might escape a direct hit, when the house shuddered as though struck by a giant's fist. Katharine ran to the front to find a great, gaping hole in an outside wall, and a cannon ball, still hot, sizzling in the parlor. Seizing the tongs, she rolled it into the fireplace. The widow poured a bucketful of water over it, and retracing her steps, dribbled more along the path the ball had charred on the floor boards.

"Better safe than sorry," the old woman muttered, as she dumped another panful of water on the gouged wall. "We can thank God 'tis no worse."

And now out of the smoke, begrimed and weary, Rachel arrived, bearing Jonathan.

"Our whole house is on fire," she whispered, giving Jonathan into Katharine's arms. "Cousin Deborah said we would be safer here. Oh, Katharine!" Her lips trembled, and her voice caught on a sob. "One—one of the bombs exploded and burned up all our clothes!"

Katharine gathered her close, smoothing her hair and wiping the tears from her cheeks. "It will be all right," she comforted. "Come out into the kitchen, and Mrs. Nolan will make you and Jonathan some hot chocolate. You will be safe here, my darling."

By tomorrow the whole town would be destitute, she saw now, and her outrage flared again. There would be no food, no shelter, no clothing—while a warehouse of wool burned up on the wharf! How dare they destroy like this! If only she could do something. To wait here, helplessly impotent, was asking too much. The wool in the warehouse! But she dared not try to reach the wharf; it would be an inferno. The house in King Street! Surely the closets there would yield something. And now she remembered Michael's books and her resolve deepened.

"I am going to King Street," she whispered quietly to Mrs. Nolan. "The firing has let up a good bit. I think you and the children will be safe now."

A burlap sack could serve as a rough mask, Katharine discovered a few minutes later, pressing one of two sacks she was carrying to her face as a shield against the acrid smoke choking her lungs and stinging her eyes almost to blindness. Back Street was little damaged, she noted thankfully, but as she turned into King Street, she gasped. Where there had once been handsome houses, now there were smoking ruins, only the brick chimneys rising above the charred and burning wood. Two or three dwellings still stood, apparently unharmed as yet by the capricious firing of the ships' guns. Among them, she saw with a leap of her heart, was the house of Edmund Winter. As she ran toward it, everywhere along the deserted street she saw the mute evidence of frantic flight—a rag doll in the gutter, a broken mirror on a pebble path, a ruffle of gold lace caught on a fence picket, a brocaded footstool abandoned against a gatepost. And the first of the ugly scavengers was abroad— a giant brown rat.

She ran up the steps of the house and then remembered. She had no key. But the door stood partly open. Katharine paused, suddenly wary. Who was inside? But as she hesitated, the ships' guns roared out again in deafening cadence here so close to the harbor, and in terror at the awful noise she plunged inside.

The house was cold and musty and dark—the drawn

blinds shut out nearly all the light. With a shiver she sped up the stairs, hating the chill shadows that somehow seemed alive. In Michael's room she snatched up a book from his night table, and in a shaft of light through a drawn shutter could just make out the title: *Midwifery*, by William Smellie. Scooping this and another three volumes into one of the sacks, she crossed to Annette's chamber to seize *The Pilgrim's Progress* and a book of Shakespeare's plays for Ben.

In the darkness of the clothespress, however, she could not distinguish one gown from another. But her quick fingers found wool and fur, and she stripped these from their pegs. In Mrs. Winter's room she snatched up another armful of garments, and thrust them in the sacks. Now neither Rachel nor Cousin Deborah need go in rags because of a vengeful king, she thought in triumph, as she slipped down the familiar staircase.

At the foot of the stairs she drew up, her heart clutching in panic. Though she could not see the light, there was a smell of candle grease. And surely she had left the door *open?*

As she moved toward it, there was a quick step from beneath the stairwell. A candle flared, and Katharine looked up into the face of a British marine.

"Lootin', m'lady?"

"No," she whispered, recoiling in terror. "This—this was my home."

His hand fell on her arm. "Ye can tell it to the captain," he said coldly, "and 'e's in the kitchen."

The kitchen was dark, too, except for the flare of a single candle that touched on Polly's copper pans above the hearth and cast into shadow a man at the table.

"This 'ere lady claims this is 'er 'ome, sir," the marine said.

The officer did not take his glance from the map he was studying. "I'll deal with her, Sergeant. Meanwhile, take the men and set a torch to every house that remains standing in this section of the town. See that the men get back to the ship, if for any reason I am delayed."

"Aye, aye, sir."

Now the officer looked up, and in the wavering light his eyes found Katharine's. She recognized him in the same instant he knew her.

"Miss Leslie!" Captain Stuart kicked back his chair and came to his feet. "In God's name, why are you here?"

"I—I could not return to England with the family," Katharine stammered. "You see I—I—"

"So it *was* you who escaped from Newgate." He nodded. "I thought on the evening of the dinner my remark drew blood. But that young doctor was so quick to cover for you—" He broke off, and coming closer, held up the candle, studying in its beam her grimy face and tousled hair. "Well, you are caught indeed. For neither can you safely accept refuge aboard a King's ship, can you?"

"Nor do I want to!" the girl flared. "How dare Captain Mowat take such vengeance? Has he no conception of the misery he causes?"

"He knows full well what he is doing," he interrupted grimly. "The burning of Falmouth will be a lesson to every other town along the coast!"

"But he is punishing those who are innocent!" Katharine recalled Rachel's anguished face. "There are many who have had no part in this rebellion!"

"The town must be taught to respect the King's laws," he said inexorably.

Recalling now his own order to put the torch to every house, Katharine turned on him. "The King's measures are too harsh!" she cried passionately. "Can't you see? They only serve to antagonize!"

"You are talking like a rebel," he snapped.

"If I am, it is such measures as these that have made me one," she retorted.

His glance fell to the sacks. "What have you there?"

"Books and clothing."

"Keep them. Believe me, there'll be little else left when we finish our work." Leading the way back to the door, he assumed again the polite mask of the officer and gentleman. "I regret that we meet under such unhappy circumstances, Miss Leslie," he said with a brief bow. "But there is no helping it."

Clutching the sacks, Katharine ran down the walk, longing to escape from such callousness, wanting nothing so much as the warmth and security of Michael's little house. She had just reached the street, when a shell, screaming over her head, struck with a sickening rip of splinters in the dwelling behind her. Whirling round, she saw a smoking hole in the wall of the dining room, the front door dangling on its hinges, and across the threshold Captain Stuart.

She could not recall what she did next. She knew only that when Michael mercifully arrived some minutes later, the unconscious officer lay in the kitchen, and she was on her knees beside him, struggling to cover him in her own scarlet cloak.

Michael threw aside the cloak and examined him quickly. "He seems not to have sustained any great injuries," he said finally. "The force of the explosion may have knocked him out." With dazed eyes she watched as he lifted a wad of cloth that looked suspiciously like a bit of her own petticoat from a wound on the Captain's head. "Or it may well have been the flying splinter that did this. At any rate it is not too serious, I hope. And you've nearly stopped the bleeding."

She groped for words. "You—you think he'll live?"

"Yes, if we get him back to his ship before some vengeful townsman kills him for his part in this day's work."

"Tell me what to do," she pleaded.

"Get the wheelbarrow from the coach house and bring it to the kitchen door." He flung her cloak up at her. "And for heaven's sake, put this on your own back where it belongs!"

She found the wheelbarrow and together they got the

officer into it. Michael had bandaged his head, she saw; in the half-light of the late afternoon the white cloth looked like damask. As the barrow struck the rough ground of the orchard, the man in it groaned, and Katharine sent an anxious glance at her companion.

"You need have no fears," he said dryly. "He'll live. But it's a little safer for all of us on this path, I fancy, than in the street."

The path ran at the back of their neighbors' houses— the Thurlos', the Waites', the Moodys'—except that there were no longer any houses, Katharine saw in frowning bewilderment. There were only shadowed, smoking beams hanging at crazy angles, and tall, lonely chimneys thrusting up to a hazy sky. The warm wind that touched their faces like a midsummer breeze came from the still smoking rubble, she realized gradually, as they struggled along behind the ruins and came at last into Fore Street. Here, except for the faint hiss as a hot piling slid into the water from the still burning wharf, there was no sound. The ships' guns had ceased firing.

Michael let down the barrow and stood up, scanning the shore. "Damn! Not a small boat in sight!" he exclaimed impatiently. "You'd think they'd make some provision for stragglers." He turned to her. "Well, wait here. There's bound to be a skiff somewhere."

Too exhausted to care about the cold and the damp, Katharine sank down on the sand. Before her, silent, shadowed in the evening light, the five ships swayed at anchor. Their mission was successfully accomplished, she thought in bitter rage. Except for a handful of dwellings, Falmouth lay in ashes.

At last she heard the scrape of a boat, and she scrambled up hastily. In another moment Michael stood beside her.

"The wheelbarrow will bog down in the sand," he said practically. "We shall have to carry him to the skiff."

Now she realized how great his labor had been, pushing the barrow with its burden along the path, for her own share of carrying this heavy, dead weight left her panting for breath like a spent runner. As they hoisted the officer into the boat, she felt her feet sink deep into the wet sand, and she shivered with the cold. With a final effort she pulled herself into the boat. Michael pushed off and began to row.

"See if there's a bucket beneath the seat," he ordered briefly, "and bail."

She found a small pail and began to slosh the icy water over the side as Michael pulled more vigorously on the oars. But it was several minutes before he hailed the ship.

"Ahoy the *Canseaux!*"

Lanterns bobbed on the deck of the warship, and Katharine, as they came in under her shadow, could smell the stench of burned powder.

"Michael Edes with Captain Stuart aboard!" Michael spoke out again. "Lower a boat! We're taking water fast!"

A boat was beside them in minutes, and three seamen took charge of the marine captain. A firm hand helped Katharine into the dry barge, and Michael joined her. They looked up at the deck of the warship.

An officer leaned over the side. "We are grateful to you, Doctor Edes." She recognized the voice of Lieutenant Clyde. "Will you come aboard, sir?"

"No, thank you."

"One question. How did Captain Stuart sustain his wound?"

Michael's voice in answer was coolly restrained, and only Katharine could see his clenched hands. "Regrettably—through the action of the ships' guns," he replied pointedly.

She stifled a gasp. Plainly this was a challenge.

But the man above her did not choose to interpret it as such. "Ah—regrettable indeed," he said smoothly. "Good night, Doctor Edes."

The barge swept them smartly to the shore, and without their burden, the walk back took only a few minutes. Shivering now and chilled through, Katharine followed Michael in blind exhaustion, clinging to his arm.

"Here we are," he said at last in a voice from which every vestige of emotion seemed to have been drained.

She looked up, and for one awful moment could not believe her eyes. The house of Edmund Winter was a twisted ruin of sagging walls and smouldering beams. Here and there flames still licked along a charred window frame or fallen wallboard. But these tongues of fire were desultory, as if sated by the feast.

Beside her Michael's voice came harsh and bitter. "Wood burns fast," he said curtly. "And it looks as if Stuart's men lost no time helping things along."

Katharine made no answer. She could find no words. With weary, dragging steps she turned away, guiding Michael to the ditch where the sacks lay—two dark shapes, warm to her touch.

"Here," he said. "Give them to me."

Gratefully she relinquished the sacks, and together they started up King Street.

In the dusky light Michael searched her face. "Tell me, Katharine," he said quietly. "Why did you come here?"

"I—I wanted to get into Edmund's house for some clothing and books," she explained slowly, finding it difficult to marshal her thoughts. "The children have lost all theirs, you know. And when I got here—" She broke off, seized with a convulsive shudder that racked her body and left her voice uncertain. "When—when I got here, I found Captain Stuart in charge of the marines who were firing the town." The captain's cold, level glance touched her again and she felt a sudden terror. "Oh, Michael!" she cried, seizing his arm. "He—he knows who I am!"

"You need worry on that score no longer." With a firm hand he guided her over a charred and smoking beam lying across the road. "Yesterday morning the mail courier delivered a letter to me from Edmund. He has apparently investigated and mentions what amounts to a pardon for you. He enclosed a note for you, and this, no doubt, will give more details. Had you been awake when I left for Windham, I would have given it to you."

But Katharine could not bring her mind to Edmund. The sickening stench of scorched and burning wool, linen, feathers, paint, and a dozen other household things swept round her in bitter waves, more intense somehow now that the noise of the guns had ceased. And the town seemed to press in on her in a nightmare of grotesque shadows, black and orange in the light of the dying flames. She was suddenly aware of the yawning space on either side of them, pierced only by desolate chimneys reaching to the sky. Not a single house on King Street remained. Those the ships' guns had missed, the marines' torches had fired.

Michael spoke again. "You will not mind sharing your chamber with Rachel, I know. Their house burned to the ground. I have offered them shelter for as long as they are in need of it."

She nodded, too disheartened to speak. The day seemed to have been born long ago, its fresh October face somehow aging in an agony of time to this wizened death mask she saw now. They turned into Back Street. Parson Smith's house was a last, flaming derelict whose swift and roaring flames seared her cheek. No one fought the fires now; it was a hopeless task. Shielding her eyes from the heat, she turned away, and drew closer to the man at her side.

"I'll be glad when we reach home," she whispered, too heartsick to grasp the full meaning of her words.

The next morning Katharine awoke heavy-eyed and feverish. Through a haze of headache she saw Rachel's small, troubled face in blurred focus, then lost it. She roused again to Michael's voice, aware of his hand, cool and light on her forehead, his fingers at her wrist.

"You have taken a chill," he said sternly. "And after last night's exposure, I do not wonder." Though his voice was severe and anxious, his fingers, smoothing her hair back from her brow, were gentle. "I shall leave instructions with Mrs. Nolan," he went on. "And Rachel can take care of you. You will do exactly as you are told, do you understand?"

"Yes," she whispered.

The herb tea, made of sassafras, prescribed by Mi-

chael and administered almost every waking hour by
Rachel, had its effect, together with the warmth and
comfort of bed rest. By nightfall Katharine felt a little
better, though her physician would grant no improvement.

"It is too soon to tell," he said soberly. "You are no
worse, thank God."

But by late afternoon of the next day, he was willing
to admit the fever broken. Katharine was bolstered happily among the pillows, her black curls swept up with
a blue velvet ribbon, her shoulders swathed in shawls.
As he came into the room, she gave him a mischievous
smile.

"You are starving me," she accused roundly. "I
could eat a horse!"

He crossed to the bed and felt her pulse. "You may
have a coddled egg," he conceded with a grin.

"And real tea?"

"Tea is only for Tories," he replied, the laughter in
his eyes belying his grave tone. "Do you think you still
fit that category?"

Though his tone was light, when he had gone Katharine pondered his words soberly. Had she ever been
a true Tory? Were her loyalties ever pledged to the
King? Michael's words, harsh in denunciation that
winter night, had been very true. She had begun life
in this new land by using her energies exclusively to
further her own selfish interests. And in her belated
efforts to prove her worth, it had been Rachel's gentle

spirit that had led her to a new discipline and self-respect.

If not a Tory, could she be called a rebel?

If to hate tyranny in all its forms was to be a rebel, then she would willingly be called one, she thought fiercely. But neither Tory nor rebel was without his own peculiar tyrannies. A rebel mob could be fully as cruel and despotic as a King's captain, she knew. It would take a great leader—who was it Michael had named—General Washington? to mold these fiery, rebellious colonists into men of responsibility and good will. Her own loyalties, she realized with new insight, were roused not by speakers, nor standards, nor slogans, but by the people she loved.

Edmund's letter, beside her on the night table, still seemed unreal—its contents incredible. Despite her deception, he had cared enough to investigate her position, and she was deeply grateful to him. She owed something, too, to Lady Blaize, who, once she had discovered young Charles secreting other of her gems, set the machinery in motion for Katharine's pardon. Mattie, the chambermaid, had admitted to a lie, Edmund wrote, confessing that her original story had been calculated to strengthen her own position in the household. There had been no word of Jay. But the anguish she had suffered through the young lord's cowardly renunciation had worn away, Katharine found. Now she no longer cared.

On the tray Rachel brought a few minutes later there was tea as well as other delicacies.

"You can have some of the strawberry jam we made together," the younger girl confided, as she placed the tray carefully on the bed. "Ben and Cousin Amos managed to save all the stores from the dry cellar."

After supper Rachel returned with Ben, who carried the two sacks.

"Doctor Edes says you and Rachel had better look over your loot." Ben dropped the sacks by the bed, gave her a fleeting grin, and thundered down the stairs.

"You open them up," Katharine directed with a smile.

Rachel drew out two of Annette's dresses, one of red wool trimmed with matching velvet, another of dark green silk. Two flannel petticoats came next, a shawl, a cloak of brown serge Annette had refused to wear, Katharine remembered, and the beaver muff.

"Oh," Rachel breathed, stroking the fur. "I've never had a muff!"

Katharine drew her close an instant. "These gifts are really from Annette," she said affectionately. "She would have loved you as much as I do, Rachel, if only she could have known you."

The other sack held a cloak, petticoats, and three of Mrs. Winter's gowns. Katharine smiled when she saw them. True to her word, Mrs. Winter had bestowed her best on friends and servants. These relics, in her eyes, were so unfashionable no lady would be seen in them.

But to Cousin Deborah, destitute of everything but the gown she stood up in, they would seem magnificent indeed.

Rachel had donned the scarlet frock, and now spun happily round, her hands deep in the muff.

"Do you—do you think it becoming?" she asked shyly.

"It is most becoming." Michael answered her question from the doorway where he stood, and Rachel, her cheeks as scarlet as the gown, came to an abrupt stop. Seeing her confusion, Michael came into the room and pulled her to him in a quick hug. "Why is it ladies are always so enamoured of a muff?" he teased, rumpling her hair.

"A muff is so soft," Rachel answered dreamily, caressing the fur again. Trailing her treasures, she departed.

Katharine pointed to the sacks. "A part of the booty belongs to you and Ben," she said with a smile, watching happily as Michael with loving hands gathered up his medical books.

"Thank you," he said quietly, setting them on a chair. Then he came to the bedside and stood looking down at her. "But do you think it was worth the risk?"

"I did not realize the danger," she said contritely. Looking up she met his gaze fully. "Oh, Michael!" Impulsively catching up his hand, she pressed it to her cheek. "I—I am so—" But she dared not express her gratitude, and overwhelmed at her blindness to his worth, and the depths of her feelings for him, she bit back her words, afraid to speak further lest she say too much.

"You are overtired, I fear." Gently withdrawing his hand, he searched her face. "It is early, I grant, but you will oblige me by retiring now," he said firmly.

"But even Jonathan is scarcely in bed!" she protested.

"Tomorrow in the afternoon you may get up and get dressed," he promised.

She gave a wry laugh. "You are sure you are not spoiling me?"

"I know I am. But you must grant me that privilege. I shall not exercise it much longer." He blew out the candles. "Sleep well."

But Katharine did not sleep. Neither her mind nor her body would respond to her bidding, she had discovered these last three days. Sometime, somewhere, her heart had betrayed her into this aching intensity, this wretched longing she could not escape. At the mention of Michael's name, all other names flew from her head. At the sound of his voice, her heart quickened. Now, she reflected in bitter irony, when she could return to the security of England, to the comforts and luxuries of London—now, when Edmund Winter offered her his heart and his hand—she wanted nothing so much as to be a part of Michael's life—to love and to be loved in turn.

And here her heart misgave her. For Michael's devotion, she knew, was to many—patients, friends, even enemies like Captain Stuart, received his help and succor. True, in her deepest moment of despair, he had rescued her, but for how many others would he not have done the same? Searching her mind, she could find no evidence that she held a special place in his heart. And certainly she deserved none, she thought in anguish. Repeatedly she had rejected his advice, in unpardonable thoughtlessness she had scorned a suggestion of marriage, however lightly given, and her few efforts to please him had been undertaken out of injured and stubborn pride.

Yet there was the joy that sometimes leapt between them in a rush of laughter. There was the touch of his hand. There was his steadfast loyalty. How much, or how little, did it mean?

The next afternoon she dressed carefully, longing to be beautiful in Michael's eyes. The rose gown was her most becoming, but since it had been Edmund's gift, she chose instead the black wool dress she had made on shipboard. With its ruffles of white lace at throat and wrists, it was very becoming, and surely its practical warmth in this stormy October weather would meet with a physician's approval. There was still a faint odor of smoke in her hair, she noticed in distaste, as she piled her black locks high, tying them with a ruby ribbon. But the whole town smelled of smoke and charred wood. The rain of the last three days had intensified the ugly odor.

At supper she learned the full extent of the damage to the town. One hundred and thirty-six homes had been demolished by the flames. The handsome new courthouse, St. Paul's Church, the townhouse, the customhouse had burned to ashes. Barns, shops, stores, and warehouses were gone. Every wharf but one or two short ones, had caught fire, and every vessel in the harbor, except two which the British had taken, had been destroyed.

"We owe our present comfort entirely to Doctor Edes," Deborah Bradley confided to Katharine. "There are so few dwellings left! Many families are sleeping in barns and haylofts—if they can find them. Think of the distress—with winter coming on! We have much to be thankful for."

"Reuben Clough was the only man in the whole town to be wounded," Ben boasted. "Our men killed some of the marines!"

"We could have made it hot for a lot more of them, had there been a plan of defense," Amos said grimly. "Half the men were on the islands, and when they did get here, most of their efforts went into saving their families and homes. That's natural enough, I suppose. But there was no real leader, and not an hour's supply of powder in the whole town!"

"Mrs. Greele saved her tavern by staying in it and fighting the flames," Michael said with a smile. "I'm told that some hot shot landed in her back yard and fired the chips near the chopping block. She took up the shot in a pan, tossed it into the street, and said to a passerby: 'They will have to stop firing soon, for they have got out of bombs, and are making new balls and can't wait for them to cool!' "

At this story they all laughed. The heating of shot so that it would ignite whatever it struck was a standard practice of the Royal Navy, Ben had told Katharine earlier. That this diabolical technique was not known to the Widow Greele in no way detracted from the story.

After supper, although it was early, Katharine withdrew from the group. The little house provided a blessed sanctuary for them all, she saw happily, but tonight she wanted the solitude of her own chamber.

A few minutes later there was a knock at her door, and to her response Michael entered.

"May I talk with you?" he asked.

"Yes, of course," she answered quickly. "Please come in."

He put another log on the fire and watched it burst into flame. Then looking up and meeting her eyes, he smiled. Katharine felt her heart leap in such swift response that a tide of red swept her cheeks. He would think her a child, she thought, furious with her weakness, and clasping her hands firmly in front of her strove for composure.

"We must make plans, and I confess the kitchen is a little crowded," he said with a wry laugh.

"Yes," she agreed. "But they are all so happy, Michael!"

"Not Mrs. Nolan, I fear. Come fire or flood, she regards the kitchen as her own sacred domain."

Katharine sat down in the rocker, and he in the straight chair opposite her.

"Do you feel that by the end of next week you will be strong enough to journey to Cambridge?" he asked.

"Oh, yes." She nodded. "Sooner if you wish."

"There is no need for haste. Amos and his wife and the children will remain here until they can rebuild their own house. Mrs. Nolan will go to Portsmouth, where she plans to make her home with a cousin for the time being."

She took up her knitting, finding that with her hands occupied, some of the tenseness subsided, and a little of the old, easy confidence returned.

"What will it be like, Michael, your work in the army?"

He shrugged. "I am not really sure. I may serve on the staff of a hospital. I may be with the troops in the field."

She ventured another question, closer to her real interest.

"What becomes of the physicians' families—their—their wives?"

"They follow, if they can, like many army wives. Of

course a captain's wife will hardly find life as easy or as comfortable as a general's."

"What shall you be?"

He laughed. "A surgeon, my dear Katharine, at thirty-three dollars and thirty-three cents a month." For a moment his gaze lingered on her. Then he spoke again. "Now tell me your plans," he said simply.

Katharine put down her knitting. It was not easy to speak of Edmund. His recent offer was so generous it shamed her. And she was embarrassed to speak of it to Michael.

"Edmund has asked me to return to England, if— if I so desire," she said with a stammer.

Getting up, he crossed to the window, and pushing the curtains aside, stared out into the wind-blown night.

"You mean he has asked you to be his wife?" he said at last.

"Yes."

For a long moment the room was so still she heard only the soft hiss of the fire. Then he turned to her.

"He is a good and generous man, Katharine," he said earnestly. "And since his return to London, an uncle has died and has left him in very easy circumstances. Believe me, Edmund is one of the few Tories who will be able to take up the old ways again in comfort and in style. You would find life there secure and safe. Here—" He spread his hands in a gesture of helplessness. "Here the war may end tomorrow or it may drag on for years."

"Yes," she said soberly. "I have thought of that."

"Then you will want me to secure a passage for you to London."

"No—no." She shook her head, beginning to see how difficult an explanation was going to be.

He stared at her. "Why not?"

Katharine rose, too, shaking out the dark folds of her gown with nervous hands as she moved closer to the fire. She turned to face him.

"Michael, I—I hold Edmund in as great esteem as you do," she stammered. "But I do not love him."

"Does that matter?"

She looked at him in dismay. Had not he himself preached the folly of a marriage without affection?

"I thought—I thought that you at least would think it does," she faltered.

"I am no longer sure what I think." Now in the fire-light she saw his face, haggard with the fatigue and strain of the last few days. "I know only that I want you safe." His tone grew suddenly harsh. "And that there will be no real refuge for you in the colonies while we are at war!"

Katharine straightened. She had come this far; she would not retreat now.

"You said once that the only real security—the—the only real contentment lies in the devotion between two people who love each other," she reminded him, trembling.

"Yes," he admitted.

"Then if I have a choice, I choose to stay here."

"Katharine!" He took an involuntary step toward her, and then drew up. When he spoke again, his voice was flat and level, and his eyes on hers were very still.

"Do you know what you are saying?" he asked quietly.

The pulse in her throat almost stifled her words. "I am saying that I love you," she whispered.

He moved so swiftly that she was like a leaf caught up in a whirlwind. She felt his lips on her hair and on her brow and on her cheek. She heard his laugh, quick and exultant, and her own, tremulous with joy. At last his hands on her shoulders relaxed a little, and he stood away from her, looking down into her face.

"From the moment I saw you in that inn—no, from the day I watched you in the garden with Blaize—I think I have loved you." Lifting her chin with a gentle forefinger, he kissed the tip of her nose. "But you," he teased, a flicker of laughter in his voice. "How long you have taken, my sweet!"

Safe and secure in the circle of his arms, Katharine returned his smile. "I confess I have been tardy," she admitted ruefully, her blue eyes reflecting the ardor of his. "But I mean to make up for it."

And she reached up to return his kiss.

ABOUT THE AUTHOR

Audrey White Beyer was born in Maine, near the scene of *Katharine Leslie*. She earned her B.A. with an English major and a history minor at the University of Maine, and has taught English at both the high school and junior college level.

She is married to Walter A. Beyer, a teacher of mathematics at Milton Academy Boys' School, Milton, Massachusetts. The Beyers have two teen-age sons, both of whom have played football, basketball, and baseball for their school.

Mrs. Beyer's first book, *Capture At Sea*, was the 1958 award winner in the *Jack and Jill* serial contest, and in 1961 she received the Tower Award for Alumnae Achievement from Westbrook Junior College for *The Sapphire Pendant*.

A NOTE ON THE TYPE

The text of this book is set in Electra, a Linotype face designed by W. A. Dwiggins. This face cannot be classified as either modern or old-style. It is not based on any historical model, nor does it echo any particular period or style. It avoids the extreme contrasts between thick and thin elements that mark most modern faces, and attempts to give a feeling of fluidity, power, and speed.

Typography and binding design by Jane Byers